Praise for *The Devil's Staircase*

'FitzGerald has written something startling, menacing and original. She shows the savagery under our civilised demeanours, which at any moment can come bursting through with dire, far-reaching consequences'
Literary Review

'A terrific, genuinely unputdownable book'
The Bookseller

'Hilarious coming-of-age romance with extremely violent, serial-killing nastiness, all in just over 200 blisteringly readable pages'
Sunday Herald

'Fast-paced grunge and gruesome horror'
The Age

'The neo-noir comic misadventures of an original heroine . . . Brilliant, shocking and unputdownable'
Sydney Morning Herald

'Lovely, sparse, elegant writing, highly original plot and ever-building tension make this book irresistible. Reading it is like stepping over the edge of a cliff, with events spiralling dangerously out of control once Bronny, a naive young Australian, begins sharing a squat with a group of 20-something travellers in London. There's sex and drugs and rock-and-roll, a whiff of true evil and a scream-out-loud finale. Wow!'
Australian Women's Weekly

'Mixing black comedy and violent thrillers is no easy task, but in this fantastic second novel Australian writer FitzGerald does it brilliantly . . . Real emotional engagement and an intelligent subtext'
The Big Issue in Scotland

'Dark, disturbing and demented – in the best way possible'
bigbeatfrombadsville

Helen FitzGerald grew up in Victoria, Australia, and now lives in Glasgow with her husband and two children. She worked as a criminal justice social worker for over ten years. She has written ten adult and young adult thrillers, including the bestselling *Dead Lovely*, *My Last Confession*, *The Devil's Staircase*, *Bloody Women*, *The Donor* and *The Cry*.

The Devil's Staircase

HELEN FITZGERALD

Polygon

First published in 2009 by Polygon.
This edition published in 2017 by Polygon,
an imprint of Birlinn Ltd

West Newington House
10 Newington Road
Edinburgh
EH9 1QS

www.polygonbooks.co.uk

2

ISBN 978 1 84697 399 4
eBook ISBN 978 0 85790 579 6

British Library Cataloguing-in-Publication Data
A catalogue record for this book is available on request
from the British Library.

Printed and bound in Great Britain by Clays Ltd, St Ives plc

For Isabel Anne FitzGerald

PART ONE

1

It was fifty–fifty. Mum had it, and had died in a pool of her own mad froth. Fifty-fifty for Ursula and for me. Our eighteenth birthday presents – hers now, mine in four years' time – would be decided by the landing of a twenty-cent piece, a head or a tail.

I tried to hold Ursula's hand as we walked through the car park and into the hospital, but she flicked me away. After that I only remember corridors, hundreds of them leading to hundreds of others. And I remember sitting in a family waiting-room for hours while Ursula and Dad talked about test results and then I remember Ursula running out of a room with her arms wide open, grinning from ear to ear. I hugged her and we twirled around in the room together. Lovely Ursula. She wouldn't go the way Mum had gone, to a moody forgetful place that reduced her to stinking incapacity and then ended her at forty.

◈

The darkness descended on the way home from the hospital that afternoon. I was certain that Ursula's test result meant bad news for me. Dad explained that this was bullshit, but I didn't believe him. As far as I was concerned, one of us had to have it, and if it wasn't going to be Ursula, then it was going to be me.

I was fourteen, and from then on my only thoughts would be of death. I would stand still for the remainder of my teenage years, looking into the air at a slowly falling twenty-cent piece.

The drive to Kilburn was a typically boring freeway drive – flat, dry and fast. There were thousands of large loud trucks speeding and overtaking tiny little family vehicles. There were hungry-looking sheep in dry fields and at least two splattered animals on the side of the road. There was a funeral parlour on the outskirts of Kilburn, a cemetery, and pigs squealing at the bacon factory in our street. There was darkness, seeping into me.

I missed out on a lot in those four years:

I never went on the Scenic Railway at Luna Park.

I never kissed a boy in case I began to love him.

I never applied for university.

I never lost my virginity.

I was already dead.

✿

Three weeks after my eighteenth birthday we drove to Melbourne. I imagined I was walking along the corridor of a Texan penitentiary. Instead of yellow-brown paddocks I saw the steel grey of cells. My Dad was the priest, rambling prayers breathlessly one step ahead of me. Ursula was the silent guard,

4

cuffed to me, leaden. I was moving towards the room I'd end in, letting it happen, not stopping it, and when I looked in the wing mirror I noticed I was eating Cheesles. I wondered why people bothered with last meals as I sucked the orange gunge from the rice ring, but then I realised that there should always be time for Cheesles because Cheesles are bloody wonderful.

Dr Gibbons had been part of my family's life for as long as I could remember, and not in a good way. As kind and as gentle as he was, he represented needles and coffins to me, and whenever his thick old frame appeared a wave of terror overwhelmed me. The wave came over me more than ever as Dr Gibbons took my blood, as he asked me loads of questions, and as he made me sign things. 'Two to three weeks,' he said. 'I'll call you.'

'Can I have a few minutes to myself?' I asked.

'Of course.'

'I just need a bit of a walk.'

I left Dr Gibbons and Ursula and Dad standing in the hospital room and walked down the stairs and then outside. I stopped at the car to write a note, popped it on the windscreen, then crossed the six-lane road.

As I weaved my way through the slow-moving traffic, I realised the darkness was going. I didn't imagine a car coming from nowhere and smashing into the side of me, sending my flattened head and twisted body twenty feet into the air and then down onto the nature strip with a thump. As I walked through the park, I didn't imagine a man in a large overcoat appearing from nowhere and either (a) pulling a knife from under his coat and slicing my throat from ear to ear or (b) dragging me into the bushes, ripping off my pants and raping me while draining the air from my windpipe with his elbow. As I walked to the other end of the park, I didn't imagine falling into the man-made lake and getting my feet tangled in weeds and yelling for help but not getting it.

I didn't imagine anything death-related, for the first time in four years.

I reached the main road on the other side of the park. The hospital had disappeared from view completely by then. I waved down a taxi.

Turning around, I looked at the trail of non-death behind me, took a deep breath, opened the door and said: 'Tullamarine Airport.'

2

I hadn't travelled further than Melbourne since I was ten, and that was only a day trip to see the penguins at Port Phillip Island. It was our first expedition without Mum, intended to cheer us up, but I remember finding the rows of tourists and the waddling penguins scarily similar and feeling a bit depressed that both had ended up in the same place doing much the same thing.

My vague plan had been to travel once I knew the result, to make the most of the years I had left, so I had the passport I'd applied for in my shoulder bag. But after the blood was taken, it hit me that I would have a pretty crap time if I knew I was dying. In fact, knowing was going to be pretty crap full stop.

I needed to *not* know. And I needed to get away now.

The one-way ticket cost $800, two thirds of the amount I'd managed to save at the Craigieburn Mint, where for six months I'd made money, literally. I bought it and ran as fast as I could to the check-in. What if Dad and Ursula found me? What would I say? What if they arrived and begged me not to go? What would I do?

'How many bags?'

It was the gruff Qantas check-in person, who had obviously been talking to me for some time, and I hadn't been listening. I'd been thinking about Dad and Ursula racing around corridors and parks looking for me, getting in the car and seeing the note I'd placed under the windscreen wiper.

Dear Dad and Ursula,

I'm sorry but I don't want to know. I won't let it take me over. It's been doing that for years and I've been wasting my life. I'm going to London to <u>live</u> and I'm going to be fine. I love you both more than ever and more than anything,

Your Bronny.

'None?' asked the Qantas check-in person. 'What do you mean, "none"?'

'I'm travelling light,' I said.

He raised his eyebrows before handing over my boarding pass and I ran, just in case they were arriving in the car park, just in case they were racing behind me to shout, 'Stop!' because stopping was the last thing I wanted to do.

✿

I was scared of heights, so I closed my eyes and remembered what my Dad had told me after forcing me to climb to the top of the old jail's watchtower. I'd emerged from the stone spiral staircase to find sweeping views and a flimsy wooden barrier that I thought would break at any moment.

'Breathe deeply,' Dad said. 'Don't think so much. Imagine you're on terra cotta.'

It had made me giggle, but it hadn't worked then, and it wasn't working now.

I decided alcohol might.

Two hours later, I was sitting on top of the world, sipping its Bacardi and Coke. I had a whole row of seats to myself and had gathered enough courage to peek out the window. Australia was going on and on beneath me. I'd lived in an Australia with boundaries – the Great Dividing Range, Melbourne, the old railway, the O'Hair farm – and had never fully understood the extent of my country. It never ended. From seat 23b, where I was sipping my seventh Bacardi and Coke, Australia was an infinite dried-out pancake.

It had taken a while to order the first drink because I had no idea if I had to pay for it or not. This was my first flight anywhere and I knew nothing about passenger etiquette. 'Would you like something?' the airhostess had asked, and I was too nervous to say yes, so I watched several rows order drinks first before being absolutely sure that the booze was free, and then ordered seven in quick succession.

'I'm Bronny!' I said to the man in 24c. 'I've had too much to drink.'

'You should never tell a man you've had too much to drink,' he said without smiling.

'Okey-dokey,' I said, returning to my seat, my face reddening. What did he mean?

'What does it mean if a guy says, "Don't tell a man you've had too much to drink"?' I whispered drunkenly to the woman in 23a.

'It means he's a prick,' she said, and I smiled, but I didn't know why, because I had no idea what she was on about either.

I went to the toilet and threw up into the metal bowl that told of each and every bottom that had sat upon it, leaving splotches of blood, wet poo still clinging to the sides, a dangling seat cover, a rubber glove. I added my story to the bowl in the form of Bacardi and Coke and reconfigured Cheesles, popped two tic tacs in my mouth, and returned to my seat. Then I fell asleep for a very long time.

A very long time on a long haul flight, I discovered, was

two-and-a-half hours. That meant there were two hours to go till the transit experience in Singapore. I was hungover, my legs were fidgeting furiously, the flat dried-out pancake below had turned to ominous black water, and then the pilot announced that we were cruising at 30,000 feet. 30,000 feet! That's a lot of feet. I closed my eyes and prayed that if there was a God could I please die floating slowly enough – without engines one, two, three and four – to write goodbye letters to dear ones before plummeting into the concrete ocean?

I was panicking. What was I doing? I had no money, no contacts, no clothes and no job prospects. I asked for paper and a pen, no longer worried about what I could or could not do as a Qantas passenger. (Judging from the group of graduates in 11 and 12 who were throwing cashews into each other's mouths from great distances I figured I could pretty much do anything I liked.) The writing material came and I began a second letter to Dad and Ursula.

Dear Dad and Ursula,

I've made a mistake. I have no money, no contacts, no clothes and no job prospects. I'll save till I can come home . . .

I tore it up. What good would it do to worry them? Anyway, it was ten minutes to landing.

I got off the plane and shuffled into the massive terminal building. People moved purposely on or beside huge moving walkways. Everyone seemed to know exactly where they were heading. I followed them, jumping on the walkway and holding the band at the side carefully.

That's when I met the man in 24c again. Hamish was his name. He was teeny, with John Lennon glasses and bright lips. I smiled at him.

'Still drunk?'

I shrugged.

'First time, eh?'

'Yeah.'

I'm not sure if he followed me, or if I followed him. All I know is that I spent my time in Transit-ville with Hamish from Toronto; who was heading back to London after going to a friend's memorial service in Ballarat. Poor girl, one minute she'd been sailing off Devon, the next she was dead somewhere at the bottom of the sea. I sat with Hamish for the next two legs of the journey and he talked me through several full-blown panics variously prompted by turbulence, an unidentified flying thing not far from the wing under my window, a passenger who held his bag (bomb) a little too tightly, a full-blown fist fight between one of the graduate cashew-throwers and a parent whose toddler got hit in the crossfire. We watched the disconnected pieces of three movies. We stood together in the passport queue at Heathrow, where to my horror Hamish informed me that I was not an EU member and would therefore have to stand in the *other* passport queue with the Chinese and Africans. Then we got the tube together to the Royal, where Hamish ran an Internet café. He'd told me the hostel was cheap, clean and good fun. Even better, he'd said, a cleaning company came round each morning to gather casual workers for the day.

✿

'We're full,' the hostel manager said, eyeing me up and down and then handing Hamish his key. 'You should've booked online.' I could have cried. I had arrived in London with 400 Australian dollars, which I'd expected would do me till I found a job, but by the time I'd arrived in Bayswater, I'd spent 150 of them. I had enough money left for three nights in a dump like the Royal, which didn't have any room anyway.

I took off my windcheater and sat on the bench, dizzy and faint. I was wearing jeans, runners and a flimsy singlet and had forgotten to put a bra on the morning before, what with the stress of finding out for certain if I was going to die.

'Oh, will you look at that,' the manager said, glancing down at me and then turning to his computer screen. 'We've got one after all.'

3

The hostel manager, an Aussie-Italian called Francesco, had thought Bronny was a boy till she took her windcheater off. She wasn't a boy. She had large unclad eighteen-year-old breasts and

12

so a room had appeared. Room 13, with the chick from New Zealand. Yes, yes.

He offered to carry her bags, but she had none, so he showed her to the room, a two-berther on the second floor. Hers would be the bed by the door.

'I don't suppose you have a spare towel?' she asked.

'On the strict condition that you come to the party tonight,' he said, captivated by several things other than the aforementioned breasts – her honest face, her natural, under-groomed hair; and her smile, which seemed entrancingly shadowed by melancholy.

It was a deal.

After Bronny had showered and dried her hand-washed pants under the hand drier, she had a nap. Her room-mate, Fliss, was still at work apparently, so she slept soundly, then went into the Internet café on the ground floor. The café was at the front of the hostel, overlooking the street. Hamish was sitting at one of the six terminals. The coffee machine in the corner seemed to be the only 'café' part of the room.

'G'day,' Hamish said, putting on a bad Aussie accent, before setting Bronny up on one of the terminals to write an email to her family.

'Ursula and Dad, I'm fine,' Bronny typed. 'I'm at a hostel in London and it's really friendly. I've already got a job. I love you!'

After finishing her email, Bronny offered Hamish the pound she owed him.

'Buy me a drink instead,' Hamish said.

He looked cute without his glasses on, Bronny thought to herself, and they headed to the basement together, both feeling as though they had been best friends forever.

✧

The party was in full swing. About twenty twenty-somethings were standing in the dining room area with MTV on full blast. Bronny did a quick scout of the room and noticed that everyone was relaxed, drunk and happy. She hadn't been to a party since Rachel Thompson's fourteenth in Seymour, which had ended at 9 p.m. with cake and lemonade. Bronny downed several beers, the first beers she had ever downed, and then introduced herself wildly to her new world:

Fliss, her New Zealand roommate, who'd just finished her shift at the pub. She was a wannabe model: dark shiny hair, deep brown eyes, ten feet tall and so thin she was see-through.

Ray the ginger Jo'burg locksmith.

Zach from Torquay in Oz, long-haired, guitar-toting, and a lover of Lenny Kravitz.

Pete from Adelaide, with huge muscles and a stern grimace to match.

Cheryl-Anne from Wagga Wagga, whose brown hair was straighter and thinner than paper and who had a three-year-old daughter: in Wagga Wagga.

And Francesco . . . Mmm . . . Francesco, with his unusual accent.

'Just suck it in!' he'd said, as Bronny sat over the bong later that night. 'Hold it in for a few seconds and then let it out slowly.'

Her cough lasted longer than is socially acceptable, and ended with arms in the air, a Heimlich manoeuvre, two glasses of water and a 'whitey'.

'Don't worry about it,' Francesco said, as he watched her sitting fully clothed under the running shower.

'Hold my hand, I'm slipping away. I can see a light.'

'I'll hold your hand, but you're not going to die,' Francesco said, as the water slipped down over her extended lower lip and onto her T-shirt. 'You're going to have waves, then throw up, then we're going to dance. And in the morning we're going to go to that place in Queensway and have smoked salmon and cream cheese bagels.'

4

After Francesco had seen me through the whitey, he escorted me back downstairs and we danced non-stop. We held hands, embraced for the slow ones, and sat close to each other on the sofa in the corner of the dining room. We were officially together, I assumed, a couple. We talked about all kinds of stuff – what he'd seen travelling, which was restaurants, what he did back home, which was eat out. I told him about work at the Mint: how some guy put his hand in the coin-blanking presser and lost his finger, and how a woman had been killed by a four-wheel-drive on the way to the MacDonald's down the road. The vehicle had swerved to miss a stray sheep – it missed the sheep, but splattered her all over Ronald. Francesco asked me if anything other than death and destruction went on at the Mint, and I said I didn't think so. My job was so boring – I was a filing clerk – that stories of injury and death were the only memorable aspects of it.

I told him about Ursula, a go-getter who always, always, got what she wanted. When Mum bought a pink and a blue Humpty-Dumpty, she got the pink one. When she wanted to go to Luna Park and I didn't, we went. When she decided to do medicine at Melbourne Uni, she did. I didn't mention her lucky test results, not only because I didn't want to talk about it, but because I realised he'd fallen asleep.

I'd never been up close with a boy before. The closest I'd gotten was at the Easter tennis tournament when Paul Fletcher and I won the mixed doubles and we had to hold one handle of the trophy each for the *Kilburn Free Press* photograph. Paul Fletcher was just like all the other Kilburn boys – a bogan with red hair and a tendency to wear ball-crunching Aussie rules shorts.

I looked at Francesco, with his groovy jeans and well-cut shirt that hadn't crinkled despite the dancing and the sleeping. I moved towards him and then lay down beside him. But I couldn't sleep. I felt overwhelmed, touching a man with the perfect amount of imperfections – a slight tummy, a large brown mole on his neck, soft hair on his arms. I looked him over, touched his shoulder, his hand. When he woke I was tingling all over. The dining room was empty except for bottles, fag butts and us. He woke and smiled at me: 'You'd better get going if you want to catch James.'

'What about the bagels?'

'I'll get one for you for later.'

James was the New Zealander who ran the cleaning company. His white van arrived outside each morning at 8.30. He ate breakfast, for free, in the hostel basement, and then collected as many workers as he needed for the day. When I arrived back in the basement after a quick wash, looking very hung-over and grotty, he was just heading out the door.

'Don't suppose you need some extra hands?' I said.

He counted the hung-over crowd waiting by the van, then said no, actually, he had enough.

I grabbed his arm before he could leave. 'Oh, please. I'm completely broke.'

❖

Later, as I scrubbed the walls of a huge bakery, I thought about each and every moment from the night before, which had been the best night of my life. I recalled the first time Francesco and I danced together, when he'd put his hands on my shoulders and pulled me closer to him. I remembered lying with him on the sofa and watching as he slept. I smiled as I collected mouse droppings with my cloth, even though James was telling me to get a move on. I sighed as I collected filthy dishes from under the counter, and only half registered that I had dropped two of them en route to the kitchen. I closed my eyes and imagined his face as I stood in the bin area with an empty rubbish bag.

'That's it!'

'What?'

James was looking at me. I'd been standing with my eyes closed for some time, apparently. I'd ignored his orders to pick up the smashed plates – which he'd cut his hand on – and I was fired.

From a cleaning job.

✧

I walked all the way to Bayswater, which took me three hours in the end. I suppose I'd formed an image of London in my eighteen years, mostly from *An American Werewolf in London.* I'd imagined scary underground tunnels, fog, grey skies, unhappy people, and werewolves. The only map I could get my hands on was a free tube map, so I walked from tube to tube, asking newspaper vendors at each one to point me in the direction of the next. Along the way, I was surprised at how exciting and clean London seemed. Orderly, beautiful, with interestingly dressed people who were, I had to admit, rather unhappy looking. I found myself entranced by the hugeness of it, by the neat perfect fruit on display in the small shops, the endless number of cafés and places selling individual slices of pizza and the gorgeous rows of Victorian and Georgian buildings.

When I got back to the Royal, I was exhausted, covered in mouse droppings, had the same singlet and jeans on that I had worn for the last three days and stank pretty much of shit.

'Francesco!' I called out as I fell into reception. He was sitting at his desk beside the owner, an elderly Polish gentleman with glasses. 'I was fired!'

'Really?' Francesco said. 'Why don't you go have a shower and we'll chat when Mr Rutkowski's finished?'

'Okey-dokey.' My lovely Francesco.

✿

I peeked into the Internet café. Cheryl-Anne was tapping away on a computer.

'Check this,' she said, showing me a photo she'd downloaded from the night before. I was dancing wildly next to Francesco, beaming. Around ten others were dancing too, but Pete, the muscular guy from Adelaide, wasn't. He was sitting, watching me.

I forwarded it to Dad and Ursula: SUBJECT – PROOF OF HAPPY STATE OF MIND.

The door to Hamish's room, a single directly off the café, was closed. I decided not to bug him – he was probably having a snooze – and headed straight up to my room.

I knew something was up when I opened the door. My bed was unmade – and I remembered that I'd made it before heading to the party – and when I looked at the shelf beside it I noticed that my shoulder bag was gone. I searched frantically around the room but it wasn't there. Bugger.

No big deal, really, I thought to myself. I could apply for another passport, and there was no hurry, I wasn't planning on going anywhere. There was only £60 in the bag, as I'd pre-paid for two nights at the hostel, and I was sure Francesco or Hamish would help me out after that. I was thinking these positive thoughts when Fliss came into the room.

'Did he make you do it in a shop window?'

'Who?'

Fliss went silent for a few seconds, bemused looking. 'Do you want to borrow a top?'

'Oh God, yes! I smell like dog shit. I was about to go to the charity shop but my bag's gone missing.'

The next hour was a lesson in hostel living. Fliss, the expert, laid down the economic law as follows:

Cider (not lager), 'e' (not cocaine), rollies (not ready-mades), grass (not hash), Kwiksave (not Sainsbury's), feet (not trains), texts (not calls), pockets (not bags), squats (not hostels).

I'd not had a best friend since prep, when I'd accepted Jennifer Simmons's kind invitation to come and play after school. It was my very first day, but I felt so grown up I said yes without even thinking about it, then ran out of the playground before Mum had a chance to find me, and skipped hand in hand with Jennifer to her house around the corner.

'Jennifer, go to your room!' her mother said when we giggled our way onto their porch.

'Do you know how to get home?' she asked me.

I don't remember her waiting for my answer before shutting the door in my face. Of course I had no idea how to get home. I was five and had only ever been as far as the bacon factory, so I wandered around Kilburn marvelling at how large everything was.

Everything was very large indeed: large trees, large sky, large red house, large horse . . . It was Mandy, one of Mr Todd's horses. Mr Todd was a leftover from the drovers' days who slept rough in the old railway. He was part of the search party my nine-year-old sister had organised:

'Mum, you stay by the phone. If the police don't ring you in ten minutes, ring them,' Ursula had ordered from her control centre at the kitchen bench. 'Dad, take the streets to the right of the main road . . . Mr O'Hair, you take the ones to the left . . . Toddy, cover the school . . . I'll keep ringing the mothers . . .'

As usual, her plan worked. Within the hour, Toddy had lifted me up onto Mandy, and led me home like a fairy princess.

I went off Jennifer Simmons after that, or she went off me, and since then I'd never had one particular friend who I enjoyed the way I was enjoying Fliss. She was absolutely gorgeous, with perfect fake tits that she offered to me like new puppies.

'Have a feel!'

'No thanks,' I said, 'I can appreciate them from here.'

She had a flippant way of doing everything, as if washing, dressing, sleeping, talking and eating got in the way of the things that really made up her life.

And she was experienced. 'Cut off your pee midway,' she advised, 'Prevents the bucket fanny.'

'Don't eat before speed,' she advised, 'or you'll cancel it out.'

'Never text back with *yes*,' she said, 'say . . . *I'll think about it*.'

'Always have a bottle of Evian at hand in case there's no way out of swallowing.'

Fliss was notching up, she said, after her engagement had ended.

'Prior to last April, I'd slept with one guy,' she told me, picking up a huge Coke bottle full of international coins and shaking it. 'One for every time since.'

I held the Coke bottle in my hand and did a quick estimate, using the skills I had honed after seven consecutive 'Guess the number of Pollywaffles in the jar' competitions at the annual Kilburn Show. There were two hundred and twenty five coins in there, I reckoned. (I won the competition twice in a row, and now hated Pollywaffles.)

'Always use a condom,' she said, taking the bottle from me and looking nostalgically at one particular coin inside.

'Khagendra from Pokhara . . . He liked chocolate cake.'

She replaced the bottle on her beside table.

'I've never had sex,' I told her.

She stared, open-mouthed, before declaring that she would TOTALLY be my mentor. We would have actual sex classes and she would teach me everything because since April last year she had been declared by 98 per cent of the men in the Coke bottle to be the best fuck they had ever had.

'What else would they say?' I muttered, accidentally.

'What?' Fliss hadn't expected her student to answer back.

'"Actually, sweetie, it was the third-best sex I've ever had."'

Fliss pointed at herself and said: 'Teacher', then at me and said: 'Pupil.'

'I'll shut up.'

'You'll shut up.'

She willowed around the room checking for clothes that would fit and suit me while giving the first official lesson in sex by Felicity James, which dealt mostly with eye position during blow-job administration (open and looking up).

Some time later I was lying in the bath, thinking about how Francesco had accidentally swept his hand across my thigh about an inch from you-know-where, when Fliss walked in. She was heading off to work. I took cover as best I could, but the bubbles from the borrowed soap-bits were few and far between and I had no face-washer.

'The house next door's been repossessed. We're breaking in tomorrow.'

I didn't answer, as I feared she would turn around and look at my naked body. I was never one for changing openly at the Kilburn pool, for creaming my legs like Angela Ross with her huge fluffy fanny. I was the one with the towel hinged to my chin as I got undressed awkwardly, desperate to maintain my dignity. Actually, looking back, I think I was most worried about seeing myself.

'Ray's a locksmith.'

I had climbed out of the tub as silently as I could and had almost managed to reach the towel with my desperate fingertips when she bounced around at me.

'Do you want a space?'

'Sorry?'

'In the squat?' She handed me the towel and turned to leave, looking back to add: 'Oh, and precious . . . If you're ever going to do it, you'll have to get more comfortable with your bod, which is fabulous by the way.'

✧

Hamish offered to lend me some money till pay-day, so I scampered off to the Slug and Lettuce. Fliss 'worked' there, but I soon realised that she really accumulated Coke-bottle coins, doing it in all sorts of grotty and impossible ways.

The cricket was on the large screen in the corner. Around 80 Commonwealthers were crowded round it, drinking, watching, and chatting. I saw Fliss leave the bar to go somewhere, and found myself scouring the room for foreigners (i.e., Londoners). There were two thirty-something men with very posh English accents in the opposite corner. I introduced myself, they bought me three Bacardi and Cokes, then asked me how much.

'We hear your friend charges fifty for full,' one of the Englishmen said, pointing his head in the direction of Fliss, who had returned to pulling pints.

'Liar,' I said to the arsehole punters, leaving my latest drink on the table and heading back to my corner of the world to watch South Africa get their 213th run.

✿

A few hours later Francesco and I shared a joint in the small garden at the back of the Royal.

'Promise me you won't do it,' he said after I'd told him about the squat. 'You promise?'

'I promise.'

I lay down on the paving stones and looked at the sky. It was weird not seeing the stars of my world. Unbelievable, really. And as I gazed at the North Star, I thought of Kilburn, the place I'd practically died in four years earlier, where I may have died all over again if I'd stayed. I thought of Ursula – school Dux, distinctions so far at uni, beautiful, but serious and oblivious to boys.

'Boys are boring,' she had asserted through her teenage years, and then, through uni: 'It's not on my agenda. I need to concentrate. And if I'm ever ready, he'd have to be unusual . . . compelling . . . He doesn't exist.'

She was a swot, burying herself in science and then medicine, and a loner, who adored the most frightening aspects of the Australian countryside – the killer wildlife and the killer weather.

I thought of Dad, fifty-three now, with hair as dark and as thick as it ever was. An engineer, whose extreme energy and love of working things out was plain to see: in chook sheds, rockeries and his home-bottled apricots. I couldn't picture what the lino on our kitchen floor looked like, because it had always been covered in the parts of our 'temperamental' dishwasher. I thought how frustrating it must have been for Mum and Dad – the GP and the engineer – the fixer of people and the fixer of things – to end up with an unfixable family.

Ursula and Dad were on the other side of the world, waking to fresh eggs and parrots. I found myself kissing my hand and blowing it to the sky.

I'd been looking forward to being with Francesco all day. I'd listened intently to Fliss's advice and had decided that I should take steps towards the whole cherry-taking procedure. By the end of this date, I'd resolved, my eye position should be open and looking up. I wasn't sure how to start if off, though, and a logistical panic stirred in me. I knew a friend who'd actually blown on the man's penis for five minutes, puffing air at it as if it was a birthday cake before he suggested she take a piece.

I knew another friend who gagged mid-way, another who got lockjaw, another who turned to lesbianism almost immediately afterwards. My nerves were getting the better of me as I waited for him to begin. And waited.

He kissed me on the cheek – ''Night *bella*,' he said, and then left. I nearly died.

⚬

'Right,' said Fliss, 'You've done nothing wrong, he's just a wank. He likes things a certain way. You need to keep perspective. Don't let them hurt you.'

'Did you get hurt?'

'What?'

'The only guy before last April?'

'Never you mind. Just keep perspective . . .Take this . . .' She popped a small white pill into my mouth . . .'and forget all about him.'

At three in the morning I found myself in the Polish club across the road, a tiny bar in the basement of a B&B, with a pool table, a bar, and some elderly Poles who I loved with every fibre of my being. They were warm and caring and had very large glasses, all four of them, and I told them so as I sat with them at the bar. Very large glasses that seemed to magnify the pain they had obviously suffered in their tragic lives.

Fliss grabbed me from the bar. 'You're scaring them,' she said. 'Your face is getting too close, you're grinding your teeth and your mouth's so dry it's making a clicking sound. Have some water.'

I drank a large bottle of Evian and swirled around the small basement room to discover amazing facts about my new friends: Cheryl-Anne ate the shells of peanuts, Zach's sister hadn't been in touch since she'd stayed at the Royal three months ago, Fliss wore no underpants even with skirts.

'BRONWYN! BRONWYN!'

I opened my eyes to Fliss, who was pouring the rest of a large bottle of Evian on my face.

'You're talking nonsense.'

'But it's incredible. So many interesting people in one tiny little room. It's like a micro-thingmy. And there's Francesco, coming in the door to get me. Francesco! My eyes are open and looking up!'

The next time I opened my eyes the sun was shining through the window of my hostel room. My head ached. I sat up and grabbed the bottle of water beside my bed, but it was empty, so I got out of bed and went to the bathroom.

'Hi Cheryl-Anne,' I said. She was sprawled in the bath. I somehow managed to fill my bottle without looking at her too much, but I have to admit that I did notice the caesarean scar across her stomach. I'd only ever seen Cheryl-Anne shit-faced or hung-over, and I wasn't sure which was worse: her obnoxious right-wing arguments incongruously coupled with an inevitable shedding of clothes, or the smells that came from her birdcage mouth the following morning.

'Hi honey, are you okay?'

'Fine, just a sore head, that's all.'

I walked out of the bathroom, breathed in some only slightly fresher air, and went downstairs to Francesco's room. I remembered seeing him at the club, but nothing much else, except that I was out of my head on drugs and had freaked out because he'd left me in the garden. I was new to relationship etiquette, much like aeroplane etiquette, and now that I was sober and drug-free it dawned on me that maybe couples didn't see each other every day. Maybe they spent alternate days together, to save it up or something.

I knocked on Francesco's door. There was no response. I knocked again. But he didn't answer.

Back in my room I received the second of Fliss's lessons. Apparently, I was showing an off-putting amount of keenness, which was verging on neediness. Also, I was honing in too soon, 'on a guy who should really shave his balls.'

'How do you know?' I asked.

Obviously, teachers don't have to answer pupils.

'You must learn to view men as sexual objects,' Fliss said. 'You don't need to like them.' With this, she handed me some clean clothes and the class was dismissed.

✿

An hour later, I walked down Queensway to the Porchester Centre. The building was Art Deco, with a gym and a pool in the main section, and the steam rooms in another. The pool and steam rooms had separate entrances and receptions but were connected by an internal door. I waited in the office at the top of the swimming pool until Pete, the heavyweight I'd met at the party in the hostel, came in to greet me. I hadn't noticed when I met him, but he looked a bit like a young Bruce Willis.

'Well, well, Bronwyn Kelly . . .'

'Hi Pete.'

Pete told me about the job I'd seen advertised in the local paper. This was my second interview ever, and I wasn't very good at it. I fidgeted most of the time, shifting my leg about nervously, worrying that he might ask me what they'd asked me at the Craigieburn Mint and that I would once again answer honestly:

'Why should we give you this job?' the twenty-three-year-old Mint-manager-man had asked.

'Because I have no ambition and no particular skills.'

'What?'

'You want me to be contented filing bits of paper eight hours a day, five days a week. For this, a candidate must be uninspired and robotic. I have these qualities. I am the person you are looking for.'

My Dad had phoned afterwards to explain to the twenty-three-year-old son of his friend (good old nepotism was alive and well) that I had an odd sense of humour, but really did have a burning drive to file invoices at the Craigieburn Mint.

Lo and behold, Pete asked much the same thing, but I was prepared this time.

'Working in such a beautiful building would be great,' I said.

'You'll be cleaning the hair out of drains.'

I looked like shit, even with Fliss's clothes on. My eyes were red, my clothes were too tight, I was exhausted from falling head over heels in love, and I was coming down from skunk and 'e'.

'It would be my privilege to clean the hair out of drains,' I said.

'Then congratulations.'

I smiled slightly then ventured, 'My first pay . . .?'

'Three weeks, I'm afraid. Can you start tomorrow? It's ladies' day. You'd be on late shift – three till ten.'

5

That night I lost my shoe. The left one. An Asics special my Dad had bought in case I changed my mind about joining the St Patrick's netball team again. I hadn't changed my mind, but I loved those runners.

'Bugger!' I said as the shoe fell from the roof and into a huge black bin at the front of the hostel.

'Shhh!' Fliss hissed, as she prised open the attic window of the house next to the hostel. My eyes were half-shut and I was crawling a centimetre at a time, trying desperately not to look down. If I looked down, I thought, I would lose my footing and end up splashed all over the pavement.

I followed Fliss in through the window awkwardly, and found myself standing next to her in a dusty attic room. We tiptoed slowly down the narrow stairs to the second-floor landing, and beheld the glorious interior of a huge Georgian townhouse. The stairs were circular, winding all the way down to ground-floor level. On each floor, at least five rooms spider-legged from a rectangular landing. We followed the steps down past the second floor, the first, and then to ground-floor level. There was no one there, just as we'd expected.

James the New Zealander had cleaned the house, he'd told Fliss. Not long after the clean, the owner had gone bust, and the house had been repossessed. I hadn't known anything about squatting, and was amazed when Fliss told me that we had the right to live in the vacant house, as long as we didn't break anything to get in. They could evict us, of course, but not with physical force, so we could change the locks and stay till the legal process was complete, which could take weeks.

And what a squat this was – gorgeous and huge. No guilt about the bankrupt owner whatsoever, and no hassles from the bank, which hadn't even bothered to try and sell it yet.

I looked up to the top floor, which was capped by a huge stained glass dome. It was absolutely beautiful.

We opened the front door and let Ray in. He was the Jo'burg

32

locksmith who'd masterminded the break-in. He'd been waiting inconspicuously on the steps of the Royal next door. 'One at each end of the street,' he ordered us. 'Whistle if someone dodgy's coming.'

We walked to opposite ends of the street and did as we were told, but no one dodgy walked past, just a few backpackers, and anyway, Ray looked so nonchalant as he changed the locks to the front door that no one would've batted an eyelid.

He whistled half an hour later and Fliss and I raced towards each other and then into the house. After we shut the door behind us, we screeched and hugged. We had a huge, wonderful house. And it was absolutely free.

✧

After Ray had finished changing the back door lock and given us our keys, we chose our rooms. I picked the one overlooking the garden on the ground floor. It was large and sunny, with a view onto the small walled patch of grass at the back, and there was a bathroom next door. Fliss took the biggest room at the front of the first floor, and Ray chose one of the rooms on the second floor.

We spent hours searching the endless number of hotel skips and eventually found an old sofa, discarded mattresses, a table, five chairs, a small television and a microwave. Everyone had sleeping bags but me, so I borrowed one from Hamish. We made a coffee table out of bricks and wood and before we knew it, we had beds, a dining room, a living room, and a house filled with all the ex-pats in Bayswater.

I got very drunk on cider. I whirled around in circles singing to the Violent Femmes, which was coming from some girl's Ipod doc. Despite my furious whirling, every-thing made sense, especially the music. Nice, nice people. Nice, nice squat. Nice, nice drink of lemonade.

I swapped clothes with Hamish my computer man, surprised that, actually, I looked pretty much the same in his jeans and T-shirt as I had in mine.

Then I went next door to the Royal. Francesco wasn't talking to me. He was doing the books, refusing to come to the door, so I buzzed and buzzed till some jet-lagged new arrival came downstairs and opened it for him. I stood at reception and pouted my lip, hoping this would be cute enough to break the ice.

'You're so selfish,' he said to me from his paper-strewn desk. 'I can't even look at you.'

Unsurprisingly, the pouting hadn't worked. Not only had I broken my promise not to break into the squat, I'd also jeopardised his job by going in via the roof of his hostel.

'I'm sorry,' I said, sobering up suddenly.

He ignored me, so I went outside to think and after a few minutes I rang the bell again. The aforementioned new arrival came down the stairs, opened the door and said in his South African accent: 'Stop ringing the fucking bell.'

I told Francesco I didn't want to demonstrate an unattractive amount of keenness.

'I'm not needy, honestly,' I said. 'I just think you're really wonderful.'

He flicked me away with a shake of the head and no eye contact.

Reluctantly I went outside again. Shit, I was needy, wasn't I? Fliss would never give me a gold star at this rate.

I was thinking I should play hard to get for a bit, maybe even ignore him, when two men in suits walked towards me then stopped.

'We'll give you six weeks,' one of the men said. 'Sound fair?'

I looked around, wondering if they had meant to address someone else.

'If it doesn't, there's always Plan B.'

I opened my mouth to say something but nothing came out, just a kind of groan, then luckily another voice spoke for me.

'Very fair.'

Pete from the Porchester Centre had come out of the party and was standing behind me.

The men nodded, then left.

'I want the big room above yours,' Pete said.

'Who are they?' I asked.

'Bank, I guess. Bloody reasonable. If it was my house, I'd go straight to Plan B.'

Pete turned to walk away.

'Where are you going?'

'To the park,' he said.

I watched his large muscular figure fade into the street. I wouldn't want to bump into him in the dark, I thought to myself.

As he passed the huge council bin in front of the hostel, I remembered my shoe. I'd been wearing Fliss's pumps all day and my feet were killing me. I ran to the bin and looked inside. It was huge and dark and filled with exceptionally smelly things. I reached down and my hand touched something sticky. Then I noticed it – a runner. It was right in the middle. Too far to reach from where I was, so I hauled myself up, my stomach leaning over the edge of the bin, and reached in . . . closer, almost . . . I could feel it . . . I got it!

I raced up the front steps to the squat and felt my pocket for my keys, but realised I still had Hamish's frighteningly snug jeans on. Cheryl-Anne and Fliss opened the door – topless. I squirmed, covered my eyes as I walked past them, and went to bed.

The following morning, when I tried to put the shoe on, I noticed it wasn't mine.

6

The shoe was blue, size five, Nike and for the right foot. Bronny squeezed it on anyway then raced to Fliss's room on the first floor to find her skinny friend lying naked beside two men who were equally naked. She looked away, scavenged a T-shirt and a pair of jeans from the floor, and then raced out of the house.

She was five minutes late and Esther – the steam room dinosaur – wasn't happy. So unhappy, in fact, that out of pure badness she gave Bronny a size 18 netball skirt and a size 18 polo shirt. Bronny looked hilarious in two right trainers of different makes and colours, a skirt that continually fell to the floor, and a T-shirt so large it was hard to spot her in it.

Esther had worked in the steam rooms for over thirty years. She was fifty-nine, thin and crinkly. She never smiled and never had reason to, because no one liked her, not even her successful children. She acted like she owned the joint – watched staff like a hawk, especially the Australians. But she needed to watch them. They took illegal drugs and had sexual orgies. For some time, Esther had taken it upon herself to rid the Porchester of such vermin, or if not, to at least make their lives miserable.

While checking for signs of drug-taking and promiscuity, Esther showed Bronny the ropes – give towel, take towel, check lockers, clean floors, clean tiles, clean drains – and surmised after half an hour that this young hussy was no different from all the others.

'You have to be fully qualified to touch this,' Esther said, opening a small metal cabinet. She explained that the cabinet housed the sauna and steam controls as well as several keys to several important rooms. She took a key from one of the hooks, and opened the cleaning cupboard adjacent to the cabinet.

Inside the cupboard were tins of cleaning fluids and rat poisons, and a cardboard box filled with lost property.

'God, are there rats down here?' Bronny asked.

'Not if we use this stuff. But you're not allowed!' Esther reminded her. 'You have to be a fully trained staff member.'

'What are those?' Bronny pointed to two large straw bundles, tied together stiffly like a broom.

'They're for *schmeissing*.'

'*Schmeissing?*'

'Some of the men smack each other with them, in the steam rooms. They're not allowed. These were confiscated the last men's day.'

Esther's eyes turned to slits as she stared at Bronny for a few awkward seconds. 'Don't get any ideas,' she said.

'About what?' Bronny asked.

The Australian had ideas, Esther could tell. From the look in her puppy dog eyes, she could sense the girl might be beating a lesbian heroin addict friend with a makeshift straw stick that very night.

❖

Throughout her first shift, Bronny's determination to avoid the viewing of private parts was commendable, despite the fact that every woman in the spa was naked. She cast her eyes to the floor in the steam rooms, to the ceiling beside the relaxation beds, to the left as she walked down the stairs by the plunge pool.

At the towel dispensary area, she found that closed was the best eye position, but once, when she opened them to answer a question from her towel dispensary seat, she found herself directly opposite a vagina. She gasped, threw the customer a towel, then quickly closed them again.

This was not a friendly environment, Bronny realised. Customers were determined to relax, relax, relax, oblivious to staff, definitely not in need of chit-chat. Apart from Esther, there were only two other staff members on ladies' days: Kate, a naked part-timer and staunch supporter of Esther, and Mitt-woman.

Mitt-woman never left the body-scrub room, a square space downstairs opposite the showers, where naked customers offered themselves to her concrete slab as if already in the morgue. Her thin body was always clad in running shorts and a singlet. She was around thirty, had curly hair, a constant grimace, and large mitts which she used to rub her customers raw, their skin falling to the floor like snow, then dampening into a thick dark coating of skin sludge. Mitt-woman never spoke. Her exfoliating gloves said it all.

✧

At 10 o'clock that night, Bronny went home to her huge house. Her keys had been lost since the whole jeans-swapping saga, so she knocked on the door and waited for one of the stoned residents to let her in. In the living room were seven other stoned faces, including the newly recruited residents – Porchester Pete, Caesarian Cheryl-Anne and Guitar Zach.

Cheryl-Anne had taken her T-shirt off and was looking at something in the middle distance. Fliss was sitting opposite Zach in her miniskirt. Zach had stopped playing *Believe* because he realised he could see what Fliss 'hadn't had for breakfast.'

Bronny was hung-over and exhausted, but her vow to *live* was an enduring one, so she somehow mustered the energy to partake in the bucket bong and in the lengthy conversation about what the conversation was about.

✿

The dream woke her at three in the morning. She was in Station Street, Kilburn. Her 70s brown brick house was in its rightful position in the middle of the street. The disused railway, where old Mr Todd kept his horses, was at one end, and the bacon factory was at the other. The surroundings had once seemed normal to Bronny – the squealing sound of pigs being slaughtered at night; Mr Todd sleeping on the ground in his dusty Driza-Bone. But in her dream, none of it seemed normal. She was running past the old railway, and Mr Todd was spookily clean, ghost-like, standing by his horses and staring at her. She was running past the bacon factory and the pigs weren't screeching, just walking slowly into the slaughterhouse. Her leaps were increasing in size as she ran, so that eventually she was bounding into the air, getting higher and higher. And just when she should have arrived home, she leapt right over and missed the house altogether, landing on the other side of it. She jumped back again, but landed even further away. Ursula was waiting on the veranda, but after a while Bronny's leaps were so large and high that she could hardly see Ursula at all.

Waking in a terrified sweat, she got up from her mattress and went to the small bathroom beside her bedroom. The house was quiet – everyone had either gone to bed or fallen asleep in the living room. She turned the tap on and drank some water, splashed her face, had a pee, then walked through the hall and back towards her bedroom. She hadn't noticed before, but there was a door in the hall under the stairs. She tried to open it, but it was locked.

She couldn't sleep. It wasn't just the residue of her nightmare. It was Francesco. She couldn't have been making it up, could she? The chemistry? How well they'd gotten on? She longed for him so badly, but now he hated her, and she didn't blame him. He'd specifically asked her not to break into the squat, and she'd ignored him.

Drifting off at around seven, the dream resumed where it had left off. Bronny could make out Ursula *and* her Dad. They were waiting for her on the veranda, but they diminished as her leaps increased. The fear woke her at the same time as a noise. A scrape, then another scrape. She sat up in her mattress, looked out into the small garden, then out towards the hall. At first she wondered if it had been the dream – the pigs, screeching at night, perhaps. She got up and walked into the living room, but the only noise was Ray's open-mouthed snore – he'd obviously fallen asleep in front of the television.

'Ray, did you hear that? Ray!'

He snorted and rolled onto his other side.

There was no noise in the kitchen, none upstairs. She came back down to the ground floor and slowly opened the front door. Nothing. She walked through the kitchen and out into the tiny garden. Nothing. She went back to bed. She was going crazy.

BANG! A huge noise this time, like a heavy wooden window shutting suddenly. Bronny jumped out of her bed, moved towards the door, and slowly opened it.

She screamed when she saw Pete. He was standing right at her door.

'Are you okay?' he asked.

'Get out!' Bronny said.

Pete stood still.

'Get out of my room!'

Bronny listened as he shut the door behind him, as he walked up the stairs, along the landing, and went into the bedroom above hers. She shivered, and she didn't get back to sleep.

7

Pete had already gone to work when I got up. Over breakfast I asked everyone how they'd slept. The casual answers indicated that no one else had heard the noises. I asked a few people what they knew about Pete. No one knew anything, but everyone seemed to like him. I didn't.

I asked Ray the locksmith (in a by-the-way kind of way) if he could open the door to the hall cupboard. 'I'm dying to know what's in there,' I said.

'No problems, soon as you get back from work,' Ray assured me.

✿

My second late shift. I arrived at 3 p.m. in my ridiculous netball skirt, watered the plant by reception, and went into the relaxation area. Esther and Kate were reading books behind the towel desk and didn't say hello. Mitt-woman remained in her room. The days were going to be long, I realised. It was other-worldly – like going back in time. Women lying reading or sleeping, donning towels then discarding them, resting and then resting some more. The digital clock behind the towel desk clicked over so slowly that 10 p.m. seemed like make-believe until it finally came.

✿

I arrived home after ten to find a parcel from Ursula which someone from the Royal had brought in for me. Inside was a photo of her and Dad on the veranda smiling widely, holding a sign that said: 'We love Bron!' There were also two huge boxes of Cheesles and a note:

Lovely Bron,
    I miss you! I hope you're having fun and being a bit

wild. You need it. But please let me know if you need anything! I'm working too hard and looking forward to doing something other than studying. It's hot and bright here and I have a large spider called Milly in my room. She says hello too.

Love you,

Urs

xxx

PS: Got the photo. Who's the hunk with the tattoos? Woah!

I stuck the photo on the wall next to my bed and sprayed the hall with an air-freshener I'd borrowed from work. Cheryl-Anne's beer farts seemed to have taken over the house. I then placed one Cheesle-ring on each finger, and ate methodically, ten at a time, in private, so that fuckers who didn't fully appreciate the magic of Cheesles couldn't intervene.

When I'd finished, I went into the living room to find everyone from next door, and some employees from the Porchester, but I couldn't see Ray.

'He's gone,' Fliss informed me.

Apparently, some girl he'd met in Thailand a month earlier had texted after breakfast to say she was in France and wanted to do 'that thing' with him. It took him ten minutes to pack his rucksack and he was never seen again. So that night, instead of checking out the cupboard and finding out more about Pete and the noises, I threw myself into a farewell party for James the New Zealand cleaner-man.

'I love this guy,' said Hamish.

We were taking turns to do pithy moving speeches.

'The nicest bloody guy I've ever met in my life,' said some girl with blue earrings.

'My soul mate,' added thingy from whatsitcalled.

'The funniest man in London.'

'We love you, mate!'

'We fucking *love* you.'

Girls took turns stroking James and crying in his arms as he showed off his one-way ticket to Auckland, waving it wildly with excitement because his girlfriend was going to meet him at the airport and they were going to move in together and it was going to be wonderful. Boys took turns slapping his back and playing a game of pin the tail on *his* donkey. I took turns (a) sucking on Hamish's bong, (b) opening my mouth for Fliss's vodka and Red Bull funnel extravaganza, (c) sniffing white powder from Zach's guitar, (d) playing *God is Dwelling in My Heart* on Zach's guitar, (e) laughing so much that my jaw tingled painfully, (f) confessing to James that – even though he had fucking fired me from a fucking cleaning job – I believed, truly believed, that I loved him more than anyone else in the room and indeed anyone in else in the entire country . . . no, the world, no, the universe.

✿

'Bronny! Bronny!' James was tapping on my shoulder. I opened my eyes. I was damp. Early morning light was shining through the window. I was lying on the floor of the living room with at least ten others and James was panicking.

'Have you seen my ticket?'

'What? No,' I said.

James started asking round, making a lot of noise, waking people up.

'Shut up James,' Fliss – who was spooning me – said.

'Fuck off!' the girl with the blue earrings said.

James shook the girl – her earrings were swinging: 'But I was showing it to you over in the corner!'

'Fuck off,' a boy said from behind the sofa, then another three in unison, from various floor locations:

'SHUT THE FUCK UP!'

'PRICK!'

'FUCK OFF, JAMES!'

So he did. He fucked off to the phone at the Royal to argue with Qantas, then with the insurance company, and then with his (ex-)girlfriend. That night, his face was so long that it clouded our enjoyment of *America's Next Top Model* – episode six, season five – and we all had to agree that James was a bit of a pain in the arse and we'd never really liked him much anyway. He moved to Earls Court not long after.

✿

I dragged myself from the floor of the living room some time the following morning. Cheryl-Anne, Fliss, Hamish and I had spent most of the weekend watching television, eating stodge, and trying several drugs that were supposed to help with coming down from several others. I didn't go near my bedroom, preferring instead to stay on the mattress in the living room, and I didn't hear any strange noises. I started to wonder if it had just been some kind of drainage or plumbing problem, especially as my room seemed to have a rancid damp smell about it.

After I dragged myself up from the living room mattress, Hamish and I swapped our clothes back – finally – then did the whole London thing: Buckingham Palace and that toyshop and Harrods. I felt so comfortable with Hamish. He was my first proper male friend. Androgynous, I'd say. Not at all pervy. If anything, he hardly seemed to look at women at all. We ate homemade peanut butter sandwiches on London Bridge.

'You want to come on the Eye?' he suggested.

'I'm afraid of heights.'

'How about the Dungeon?'

'I've heard that's really scary.'

So instead we talked about rural Victoria, where his good friend had lived. He'd been in Ballarat before we met on the flight, and found its colonial buildings and gold-mining history really interesting.

'I found two dollars' worth of gold at Sovereign Hill!' he said.

'You realise they sprinkle it in each morning?'

'I know. Oddly, that didn't make it less exciting.'

He was the first Canadian I'd ever met, but if he was anything to go by, then Canadians were the most down-to-earth, easy-to-be-with people in the world.

When we got home from sightseeing, Francesco was cooking something extravagant in the kitchen and talking secretively to Pete. They were like bitchy schoolgirls – obviously talking about us. I ignored both of them and went back to watch television with my good friend Hamish.

At around four in the morning we ran out of grass. I volunteered to accompany Hamish on a visit to Bobby Rainproof, who apparently based himself at the Polish club across the road.

'So what does he do?' I asked Hamish as we crossed the road.

'He's a drug dealer.'

'Oh.' I knew we were going to buy some stuff from him and all, but for some reason I didn't equate that with drug dealing. After all, I was an eighteen-year-old from a good – though genetically fucked – family.

Bobby Rainproof was sitting with three elderly Poles, who moved away from the bar when they saw me approaching.

'What's up with them?' I asked Mr Rainproof.

'Apparently you gave them nightmares,' the young guy answered.

'You don't look like a drug dealer,' I said.

'Shhh. *Dio cane!*' Bobby's expletive and accent indicated that he had been christened Roberto Rainproofo. 'You want to get us arrested?'

He took Hamish and me into a back room where some more elderly Poles were playing poker. I wondered just how many elderly Poles with glasses there could be in London. We then followed him into an even backer back room where three large bars of dark brown 'soap' were laid out on a small table.

'You not got any grass?' Hamish asked.

'Maybe next week,' Bobby said.

He chopped some of the cannabis and wrapped it in cling film. Hamish and I watched, entranced, as he ripped a piece from the industrial-sized roll and laid the plastic on the table. He did an extremely neat and thorough job of wrapping it. Hamish handed him thirty pounds and put the stuff in his pocket.

'*Grazie*,' Hamish said, and we followed the good-looking twenty-something from La Spezia through the back-back room, the back room, and the bar. He double-kissed us then we crossed the road to our eagerly awaiting best friends.

✧

Hamish, Fliss, Cheryl-Anne and I went to Oxford the next day. We got a bus, spent the day in the pub, then came home to smoke some more of Roberto Rainproofo's most excellent shit.

8

Esther wasn't happy when I was declared Employee of the Week. She hadn't been happy for days. First, because a uniform that fitted me had mysteriously arrived at reception during my third shift. Second, because people seemed to like me. Third, because she was a fuck-face. I saw her snarl as Centre Manager Nathan put my photo on the notice board in the main reception by the gym.

It was a big deal, Employee of the Week. It meant two things: a fifty-pound bonus, and that Esther would hate me even more.

I saw Esther whisper to Kate. They enjoyed whispering, those two. They despised the cheerful demeanour that had helped get me the bonus and a high-five from boss-man Nathan.

Boss-man Nathan wore a suit. He was about thirty-five, new, and keen on team-building, staff appraisal, forward thinking, mission statements and bottom lines. He liked me because whenever his female minions came to spy for him, I was always either scrubbing something, or being polite to customers. Kate and Esther, on the other hand, were either reading or chatting to each other. In truth, my hearing and fitness were better and I had tuned into the creak of the internal door between the steam rooms and the pool. As soon as it began to open, I instantly sprang into action.

✧

I'd never been on a pedestal at work before. At the Craigieburn Mint, I'd gone in each day at nine, sorted paperwork, filed it, and then gone home at five. I had delivered what they'd asked – robotic diligence – surrounding myself with twelve grey filing cabinets. No one knew me very well, and I'd never gotten so much as a Christmas bonus. So I felt excited at my new title, proud of myself. While the job was mostly very tedious, there were things I really enjoyed about it. I liked watering the once-dying bamboo palm beside the reception booth, and seeing how it responded to my love and attention. I liked the satisfaction a clean shower gave me, liked seeing the contentedness of the rich Arab woman who preferred two towels not one, and the smell of a freshly bleached floor. I liked how my skin felt afterwards – smooth and soft from the steam. And I liked that I felt safe, bubble-wrapped in female-only calm.

✿

The day after my elevation to Employee of the Week the atmosphere in the steam rooms seriously deteriorated. Esther had always kept an eye on me, but now she watched my every move, and gave regular whispery reports to Kate. At one stage Mitt-woman even made eye contact with me. She'd never done this before. Her eyes were always down as she walked into her room, down, down as she scrubbed her clients. A snarl, I'd call it, and then a knowing nod to Esther. I tried my best to get on with things, even tried making conversation with the rich Arab woman who liked two towels.

'You live close by?' I started.

'No,' she replied.

After my shift I escaped to use the free facilities, which was the only real perk of the job, and something I did as often as I could. The pool and gym helped me sweat out the unhealthiness of life in the squat and, even better, made me very toned. In fact, I had recently copped myself cleaning the full-length mirrors opposite the showers and noticed how good my legs looked. Shapely, muscular, like someone else's altogether. I took to cleaning these mirrors more than necessary in an attempt to convince myself that these very excellent legs actually did belong to me.

I did forty lengths of the pool, got showered and changed, and walked past the gym, where Pete was doing bench presses. He had shorts and a singlet on, and his upper arms and shoulders were covered in tattoos. He caught my eye without flinching and then resumed a grimace-ridden bench press. He scared me.

When I saw Nathan I smiled, but he didn't smile back, or give his precious Employee of the Week a high-five. He beckoned me upstairs with an unhappy finger then sat me down and fired questions at me.

What time had I left the steam rooms? How long had I been swimming for? Did I remember giving a towel to a rich Arab woman? Did I notice she had a red handbag? A brown leather wallet? Three hundred pounds in cash and three credit cards? Which locker had I used?

Pete came into the room at this stage and sat beside Nathan. He'd just heard about the alleged incident, he said, and wanted to be present during the enquiries. Kate and Esther kept their heads down as I told Nathan that I did not remember the bag and that I had no locker. They almost managed to suppress their smiles when Nathan said he would get a female member of staff to search locker number 78 because Kate had sworn blind that she had seen me put something in it earlier that afternoon.

Frozen in fear, I stood by locker number 78. Kate and Esther watched as one of Nathan's female underlings opened the door.

It was empty.

Kate and Esther looked at each other, confused. I sighed with relief then shook my head at my accusers. Why had they tried to set me up? What on earth had I done?

'Are you okay?' Pete asked as I walked out of the steam rooms and then out of the front entrance.

'Fine,' I said, not meaning it, but not wanting to talk to him either.

On the way home, I felt the weight of being alone. If I was charged with a crime, who would vouch for my character?

✿

When I saw Francesco hovering outside the house, I squirmed. I didn't want him to see me upset and I couldn't tolerate another barrage of well-deserved insults. But he'd had time to think, he said, and had forgiven me. He even apologised for being so rude, hugged me, and asked if we could maybe start over.

'Let me take you out for dinner,' he said. 'Please?'

9

Bronny was relaxing in the ground-floor bath and had just finished shaving her underarms, her legs and her bikini line. The date with Francesco was in an hour, and she was excited. Fliss had given her some bubble bath, which she sank into; eyes closed, and listened to the sound of wet nothing.

Thud thud thud. A womb noise, dull and alien. She came out of the water, opened her eyes . . . And there he was again. Standing over her.

'Jesus!' She yelled, knees to chin, arms cocooning.

Pete yelled too, then covered his eyes in a pathetic attempt to pretend he hadn't meant to see her naked. He left the bathroom with a feeble apology.

Bronny dried and dressed herself, then banged on his door. He opened it sheepishly, unprepared for the assault – not only words ('arsehole', 'creep', 'police') – but also a spectacular and well-placed cheek-slap. She then left to prepare her body for the losing of her virginity, which she'd decided would happen tonight.

✧

Francesco was waiting at the wine bar. He was wearing jeans and a striped jumper and was sipping a glass of red wine. He looked different outside the hostel – less attractive somehow, but after Bronny drank two pints of Fosters he got better-looking again. They apologised to each other, and Bronny told him about the noises.

'You're from Hicksville,' he said, 'Probably just getting used to the big smoke . . . That, or you need to stop smoking ganja.'

They went back to the squat after closing. The others were in the living room watching a repeat of *Eurotrash* and laughing very hard while taking turns with the bucket bong.

Bronny sat on a mattress beside Francesco and felt his knee touch hers. She found it hard to breathe when he held her hand, even harder when he touched her lower back and rubbed it slightly. Images flooded her. This was going to be it. Could it be happening, really?

He swooped in without any warning at all, like a Kilburn magpie, just suddenly there, pecking. She was taken aback, and found the feeling of his mouth rather odd – were those his teeth? Where did his lips begin and end? She forgot everything Fliss had taught her about how to prevent sloppy-kiss-rash and how to discourage lizard-tongue without giving offence, and began what she had practised on the hand basin next to her Kilburn toilet. Face at 10 or 2 o'clock; mouth half-open; tongue relaxed, wet and wide; tongue movements slow, gentle and irregular; nose-breathing soft or not at all.

But it was hard to focus and at one point she wondered if she had bitten him as his hand reached for a private place. In the end she was so desperate for air that she pushed him away and laughed, looking around the room at the people who were still there. She giggled nervously, expecting him to suggest they go somewhere else, but he didn't. He pecked her on the lips again then went for the full magpie swoop. Bronny kept her eyes open this time, watching as four people flicked between her first kiss and Channel Four.

'I'm going to bed,' Pete said a little curtly from the sofa opposite Bronny and Francesco. Bronny abandoned the kiss, gulped some overdue air and watched as Pete walked out of the room.

'I'd better be off too,' Francesco said.

'What?'

'See you tomorrow.'

And Francesco left, just like that: without taking his grey and white striped jumper, or Bronny's virginity.

10

Oh shit, the darkness. It was lying on me. I sat up when I felt its heaviness on my chest, took some deep breaths, and then went to the bathroom for a glass of water.

When I turned off the tap, it began to shake – huge tremors, deafening thumps. I raced from the bathroom into the hall and upstairs into Fliss's room where, to my horror, she was having the sex that I was supposed to be having. It was Zach lying underneath her, not strumming his guitar, but something else that made Fliss say pussycatpussycat over and over. They didn't hear me or see me, so I ran to Cheryl-Anne's room on the second floor. We linked arms, both of us half-dressed and terrified, and tiptoed down to the first floor. We stopped and listened in the hallway, but the noise had gone.

I must be going mad, I decided. I'd taken a lot of drugs in the last few days, and had little sleep. I'd changed my diet, my routine, my everything. Maybe I was hallucinating.

When Pete's door creaked open in front of us, Cheryl-Anne and I jumped and screamed.

'What's up?' he asked in his usual monotone.

'Did you hear the noises?' I asked.

'Nope,' he said, then checked out the first floor and ground floor as we crept behind him.

'Try that door,' I said, pointing to the door in the hall.

He went up to his room, came back down with some kind of tool kit, and fiddled with the lock. After about five minutes – during which time there were no scary noises whatsoever – he smiled at us, raised his eyebrows, and opened the door.

It was a cupboard. A boring cupboard with old rolls of wallpaper, cans of rusty paint piled high, an old record player and some records.

'You're going a bit nuts,' Cheryl-Anne said.

After giving the house the all-clear, Pete made us a cup of tea, and sat with us in the kitchen till we were giggling happily.

'You need to stop taking that shit.'

He was right, the dope was obviously messing with my head. He went off to his room, leaving us to drink our tea.

'What I would do to lick those quads!' Cheryl-Anne said after he'd gone.

'Really?'

'He is *gorgeous*,' she said. 'Enigmatic.'

Hmm.

✧

I almost kept the darkness away that night in bed. Almost ignored the feeling of sinking, of weighing a ton and being too tired to sleep, too sad to cry. Almost. But the screeching noise started. It felt as though the noise was inside my head. I put my hands over my ears. I put my makeshift pillow over my head. I scrunched my eyes, hummed, then tried to think about nice things: Francesco . . . (teeth, didn't quite work) . . . Chocolate . . . (seemed to have ants crawling around in it) . . . Ursula . . . Ah, that worked . . . Dad . . . Oh . . . My Dad, my Ursula. I would write to them tomorrow, tell them I loved them.

I felt a little calmer, removed my pillow from my head and tiptoed to the window. I opened the old curtain and peered into the darkness, unable to see anything. I relaxed a little, and then a grey tabby cat bounced up at my window and meowed an on-heat meow, a terrifying baby squeal. I jumped backwards and held my racing heart until my breathing slowed down. It was just a cat. The screeching noises were coming from a little grey cat. Thank God!

I wasn't calm enough to sleep, so I went back into the hall and opened the cupboard door. It was cold in there. It gave me a shiver. I picked up the old record player and a couple of Beatles records and took everything into my room. Dad used music to relax. He'd set his stereo up in the shed and play classical music very loudly till he felt better. Mozart had floated over our garden for a long time after Mum died.

I set the player up under the window and switched it on. I blew the dust off a record, placed the needle on the vinyl and lay back on my mattress. It crackled away cheerfully, and when the song ended, I put it on again.

I picked up the needle and played it a third time, then a fourth, and during the last repeat, the needle jumped: at the *please help* part, bouncing back down to repeat the words.

It had jumped high off the vinyl, a centimetre or so, then played through to the end of the song. Or had it? Pete was right, I needed to stop smoking skunk.

11

Pete craved space. The closest he could find was Kensington Gardens at the top of the street. After he finished work at the gym, he walked along Queensway, past Whiteley's shopping centre and the cafés and pubs, into the parallel Queensway

Terrace, past the Royal and the squat and up to the end of the street. He crossed the busy road and entered the gardens. He noticed Bronny almost immediately, reading a *Lonely Planet* guide in the shade. He thought better of going over to her. She'd made it pretty clear how she felt about him. Instead, he walked past cricketers and sunbathers, past the pond and statues, and into Hyde Park.

It wasn't space as he knew it, but it was something. He found a reasonably empty piece of grass and lay down on it. He closed his eyes and imagined himself at home. He thought back to the time he'd been driving along Eyre Highway, the 1,668-kilometre stretch of straight treeless road that cuts its way along the Nullarbor Plain. He'd been sitting on the roof of a Jag, sunroof open, feet on the steering wheel, brick on the accelerator. The land around him was yellow, empty and endless, just as he liked it. He wasn't one for all those English trees and hedges that emptied the desperate reservoirs. He liked it dry. He'd had his sunglasses on and his arms outstretched to embrace the land. He'd breathed it in. His beloved and beautiful Australia.

Pete inhaled as he lay on the English grass, trying to smell home: eucalyptus and dust. He tried to hear home: kookaburras and parrots, to feel home, happy.

'I want to ask you a favour.'

The Australian accent felt like part of his daydream. Low and smooth and drinkable. He made an 'Mmm' noise, then opened his eyes and realised the voice was real. He sat up.

'Stop jumping out at me.' Bronny was standing over him, her book in hand.

'Have I been jumping?'

'Yes. In private places.'

'You make noises . . . screaming or something. You wander around at night.'

'You mean I talk in my sleep?'

Pete mimicked a high-pitched, distressed voice: *I'm trying I'm trying I'm trying . . .*'

'No! Really?'

'Wait for me Ursula, Dad! You're so small!'

Bronny hadn't really spoken to anyone since she arrived, not properly. Conversations had been about hash, mostly, and sometimes hair removal. She was aching to talk. It surprised her that this large elusive man was the one she wanted to talk to. She sat down beside him on the grass.

'That's my nightmare.'

'What is it you're trying to do?' Pete asked.

'Get home. But I end up running too fast and kind of bounding too high. I end up getting further and further away.'

Pete smiled at her. He understood.

'I miss Cheesles,' Bronny said.

'The beach,' Pete said.

'Trams.'

'People who say hello.'

'Chocolate teddy bear biscuits.'

'Is Ursula your sister?' Pete asked.

'Yeah, she's twenty-two. She's the double of Dad.'

'Is she the one in the photo in your room?'

'When did you see that?'

'That time I came in to see what all the noise was . . . She looks like you,' Pete said.

'She's the lucky one. Got the gorgeous hair and the brains and the legs that go on.'

'She's just like you.'

'No, I'm the double of Mum.'

Bronny didn't tell Pete that her Mum had died eight years earlier. She didn't describe her most vivid memory – the choking sound, running into the bedroom, her Mum yelling at a ten-year-old stranger at the end of the bed: 'Who's that? Get her out of here!' She didn't tell him that she hadn't cried when she died, or at the funeral, or when she visited the cemetery, or ever since. She'd taken the tears and rolled them into tiny balls of stone. She could feel them sometimes, tiny hard balls of stone in her stomach.

'She must be very beautiful,' Pete said.

'Mmm.' Before it all got horrible, her Mum *was* beautiful.

Bronny did tell Pete other things, though. She told him about the bacon factory where she'd buy cheap rashers once a week, ignoring the yards filled with sad-looking pigs outside the building and the boiling cauldrons of them inside.

She told him about the day she went to Luna Park in St

Kilda. Ursula had been begging to go for years, and their Dad finally took them and bought them an all-day pass.

'I was fifteen,' Bronny said, going on to tell him that not only had she argued the whole way in the car – 'I don't want to go! I don't want to go!' – but she'd also refused to go on any of the rides.

'I sat underneath that huge mouth with my arms crossed,' Bronny said.

When her Dad came out for the twentieth time, begging her to cheer up and try and have some fun, she agreed to have a snow-ice cone. As the woman poured blue liquid onto the ice, Bronny noticed Ursula lining up to go on the famous Scenic Railway roller-coaster. She ran to the queue to stop her, but by the time she got there Ursula had gotten in the front carriage. Bronny jumped the barrier, screamed for her to get off, because people die on these rides! They get stuck upside down and die! She yanked at Ursula's collar while the attendants rang security.

'We were banned for life,' Bronny told Pete, 'Ursula didn't speak to me for three weeks.'

Bronny told him about scraping by at school and working as a filing clerk at the Mint. She could tell he was wondering why she was such a low achiever compared to the rest of the family and offered her excuses before he asked.

'I never saw the point in going to uni. Why bother?' she said.

She told him about how homeless Mr Todd always seemed

happy. Caked in the dirt he'd slept in for years, he seemed as much a part of the landscape as the old bluestone jail Ned Kelly's father had reportedly escaped from.

'What happened to Mr Todd?' Pete asked.

'Some do-gooder got hold of him and put him into sheltered housing. They gave him a bath, washed the dirt off, and he died.'

'Just like that?'

'I think it held him together, the dirt.'

'I want to show you something.' Pete pulled her from the ground. They walked to the other side of the park, crossed a road or two, strolled past shops and cafés and then houses and small gardens. Pete stopped when they arrived in a back lane behind a row of huge white town-houses.

'Smell,' he said.

Bronny closed her eyes and inhaled through her nose. 'Eucalyptus.'

'I reckon some homesick Aussies like us planted it.' Pete pointed to the huge eucalyptus tree in the back garden. Some of the branches overhung the lane. He reached up to one and pulled some leaves from the tree.

'One day I want one of these in my garden,' he said, placing the leaves in Bronny's hand.

They walked for a long time that day. First to a garden centre, where Pete bought Bronny a small eucalyptus tree – about a foot high.

'Which pot?' Pete asked her.

'Yellow.'

Pete carried the tiny tree in its sunny yellow pot through London, stopping en route to show her something else that interested him.

'Do you know where we are?'

'No.'

'Bucks Row. PC John Neil found a woman lying on her back right here, her clothes were pulled up, blood was oozing from her throat . . .'

'Ook!'

Pete put the pot down and spoke excitedly.

'The first proper serial killer. At least the first one people read about, followed, like a celebrity. Jack the Ripper. Five women, they reckon, mutilated . . . some had their organs ripped out.'

'Shut up!'

Pete put one hand on Bronny's throat and the other around her waist, acting the story as he relayed it.

'He grabbed them, lowered them carefully to the ground, then slit their throats.'

Bronny was looking up into Pete's eyes as he held her arched back. If this was a dancing situation, it would have been quite romantic.

'Then he kept a bit, like a kidney!' Pete said.

'Shut up!' Bronny managed to get upright, then she ran away. Pete picked up the pot and ran after her, giggling.

✿

When they got back to the park, they lay on the grass. One of them lay down first. If you'd asked them later neither would remember which one it was, but they lay down on the grass and shared the same view of the same sky, silent and comfortable. When Bronny woke to the noises of the evening, Pete was still in the same position.

'I've just officially slept with a man for the first time,' Bronny said, stretching.

'You're kidding?'

'Nup.'

'I take it you've fucked a guy, though?'

Bronny hit him in the stomach and he doubled up, first in pain, and then in laughter. They walked back to the squat together without talking. Some chemicals had unexpectedly arrived on the scene, which meant they were silent, but no longer comfortable.

12

I was going to be late for my second official date with Francesco. I wasn't so sure about him for some reason – well, I knew the reason. It was Pete. He was nicer than I'd thought, and I'd just spent the most wonderful day with him. But he was a bit weird, especially all that serial killer stuff. However, I needed to see Francesco again because I was still a virgin and in sexual lesson number two Fliss had said that under no circumstances should I relinquish my flower to someone I have strong feelings for.

'You need to be in control,' she'd told me. 'Total control.'

'Are you really into Francesco?' Pete asked me as we walked down Queensway Terrace. I smiled.

'Yeah, well kind of. Why?'

'Nothing. Just, he's not the serious type, y'know.'

'I've spent far too long being serious.'

We were about to cross the road to the squat when I saw two little boys sitting on the step of their main door flat. One of them was about seven years old. The other about five. They still had their school uniforms on and they were staring ahead, their hands holding up their heads. Just staring, cute as buttons, but sad. The youngest had curly blonde hair that had probably never been cut and a Band-Aid on his knee. His bottom lip curled outwards to emphasise his grumpiness. The older one had short dark hair and a serious face.

'Hey you guys!' I said, before crossing the road.

'We're not allowed to talk to strangers,' the curly little one said.

'I'm Bronwyn. I live over there . . . So I'm not a stranger.'

'Strangers are people you wouldn't let hold your ultra rare cards and I wouldn't give you any of mine. I've got five.'

'Four,' the older one said, rolling his eyes.

'Dr Who,' a man said, appearing from the front door behind the boys. 'He's obsessed.' The man patted the older boy on the head. 'Any sign?'

The boy shook his head sadly. 'He's not coming.'

'He will, he always does, eventually . . .'

The man put me in the picture: 'Bobby, our cat, he's a gallivanter.'

I surmised that Greg was their Dad. He was slim and gorgeous, but also a little sad looking. As we did introductions, I noticed that Pete had crossed the road and gone inside the squat.

I turned to the youngest boy again. 'I'm very pleased to meet you and if ever you feel confident enough I would love to see one of your ultra rare cards, from a distance obviously. No holding.'

'I'll think about it,' the curly-haired boy said. The older one stood up excitedly; the cat had suddenly emerged from behind me. It was the same cat that had jumped at my bedroom window. It meowed innocently.

'Oh hello,' I said before heading home. 'He was in my garden last night!'

As I shut my front door, I looked back to the flat across the road. The boys and their Dad were holding the cat, but still sitting on the step, staring sadly.

✿

After getting ready for my date, I looked out my bedroom window and saw that Pete had put the yellow pot with the tiny tree in the garden. It made me smile. He was cooking Thai chicken curry when I went into the kitchen later. I had, once again, prepared myself for a night of lust, and had one of Fliss's ridiculously revealing tops on.

'Hello mister,' I said, opening the back door and checking my little piece of Oz. 'Thanks for watering it.'

I tasted the green curry, which was very good indeed. It had basil and coconut cream.

'Yum,' I said. 'Can you save me some?'

'Where are you going?'

I raised my eyebrows with a 'never-you-mind' and waltzed out of the kitchen.

✧

It seemed pretty obvious after the second date with Francesco that I would never lose my bloody virginity. I felt like Batman with his ticking bomb, running around trying to get rid of it, but finding nowhere to put it. Over dinner, I picked at food as Francesco yacked on about some restaurant in Scotland where you could choose your oysters from the loch. I couldn't listen. It was boring, and I had only one thing on my mind, a mission.

I hadn't had a mission in a while. Like when I was nine and St Patrick's were to play the Broadford Minis in the grand final. I was centre, a furious little runner, and I'd never wanted anything so desperately in my life. I drew diagrams on a flipchart Dad brought home from work, deciding which moves would disarm my opponent, Kylie Dalkeith, and which throws would clear the tall defender who'd just moved south from Puckapunyal.

I practised dodging in the garden. I ran to school and back each day to keep fit, and prayed. Please God, let us beat the Broadford Minis!

We lost. 23–21. I cried right up till the night I won Best and Fairest.

Since giving up netball at fourteen, my obsession with it had struck me as alien and pathetic. But here I was, obsessed again: with scoring a no-strong-feelings sexual encounter.

'I just think we should take it slowly,' Francesco had said after another boring dinner that he'd paid for. 'I like you too much.'

I'd had three pints of lager, all of which seemed to have gone to my thighs as much as my head, and felt rather stroppy. I wanted to do it and I wanted to do it that night.

'Screw "slowly". Just take your trousers off.' I was actually pulling at his zip in his hostel room and he was stopping me with his hand. What the hell was wrong with him?

'Let's talk about this tomorrow, over dinner. I've got indigestion.'

He pushed my hand away and opened his bedroom door for me to leave.

'I don't want dinner, I want sex!' I yelled. The door was wide open and Hamish, my computer friend, was standing in the foyer. He winced.

'Bronny! Wait!' Hamish said, following me out of the hostel.

'What is wrong with me?' I asked him. He sat down with me on the front step.

'Nothing. You're perfect. He's actually being very decent.'

'Who wants decent?'

'You do, believe me. And there's plenty of time for all of that. No hurry. Enjoy yourself.'

'I'm scared I'll never lose it.'

'You need to lighten up.'

I took Hamish's excellent advice. We went to the squat, smoked two bucket bongs and ate at least seven white bread, real butter and crunchy peanut butter sandwiches. Hamish and I had finished the loaf when Pete came into the kitchen. He looked unwell.

'Did you save me some?' I asked him.

'What?'

'Green curry.'

'Oh, no.'

'Lucky escape, I reckon. You look a bit peaky.'

'I'm fine,' he said, walking out with his glass of water.

✿

I had a bonkers idea after Hamish left. It came to me as I stared at the living room wall: wouldn't it be fun and – yay – necessary – to tiptoe up the stairs, open Pete's bedroom door and yell 'BOO!'

He was lying stark naked on his mattress. He made no attempt to cover himself up, and I made no attempt to stop staring – at his face, at his torso, and then at his bits. I'd never seen bits in real life, and – in Pete's case – *lots* would have been a more apt description. When I finally looked up towards Pete's upper half again, he stretched his hand towards me and held it there. There was a peanut stuck in my molar. I picked it out with my tongue, then turned, walked out the door, and shut it firmly. I stood against his door in the hall, breathless, and a little numb.

'Ow!' Pete had opened the door while I was still leaning on it. I fell backwards into his arms. As I righted myself and turned around, I was relieved to see that he had put on his shorts.

'Are you okay?'

'Mmm, fine,' I gulped, finally prising my hands from his inked biceps.

I was suddenly awkward around this guy. Not like with Francesco, who, to be honest, probably bored me into relaxation. During our sexless dinner dates, Francesco had only ever talked about food. He was a rich boy, I realised, happy to eat out most nights, unlike his skint fellow travellers who lived on pot noodles, toast and peanut butter, and pasta and pesto. His parents had slaved away in the restaurant business and left him with a love of everything culinary.

'My family are from Umbria,' he'd explained during our last date. And before he'd even ordered a starter he'd decided: 'For breakfast tomorrow I'm going to have poached eggs!'

So with Francesco there was indigestion rather than sexual tension.

Not so with Pete.

Escorting me into the living room to 'chat', Pete fluffed the sofa cushion for me. He then sat beside me and I wished he hadn't because it was altogether too close. The sofa was old and soft and we both sank into the middle and touched each other from the leg all the way up to the shoulder. I stretched my torso in the other direction. I did the buttock-lift. But it didn't work. He was too heavy, the sofa was too squidgy, and the torso and buttock refused to be diverted from their touching positions. To make things worse, I had turned my neck at right angles to listen to his 'chat' and it had locked. If I moved my head, I pondered, as I breathed carefully through my nose, it might just fall off. So I didn't move it. Instead I said yeah a lot while he told me about some flat town near Adelaide, which he loved, and which I thought sounded bloody awful.

When Pete finally said goodnight, I managed to remain upright on the sofa until he disappeared, and then fell down sideways, my neck still ninety degrees from where it should be.

○

There were no noises that night. I had the first decent sleep since I'd moved in. The next day, I arrived for my shift at work, watered the bamboo palm as usual – I seemed to be the only person who ever did – and wrote another letter to Ursula.

Dear Ursula,

I'm sitting at a desk in the Porchester Steam rooms, which is where I work forty hours a week. I hand people towels and clean the hair out of drains. There are naked women everywhere.

Have you decided to forgive me? Do you understand? I can't – won't – talk about you-know-what, but I'm not hiding from you or Dad anymore. I'm just trying to have some fun, and it's kind of working except for the naked women everywhere.

God . . . Kate and Esther are talking about me from the chairs across the way. They can't stand me, the old bags. I was made Employee of the Week by the knob-head manager, and they are so jealous. Kate, the flabby white thing has boobs that reach the floor when she sweeps it. And Esther, she's an arse-licker and I hate her.

I've met a boy. His name's Francesco. He manages the hostel next door to my house and likes eating out. There are so many Aussies here – there's one guy called Pete, but I'm not sure what I think of him yet. (He's the one in the photo.) And my new best friends – Hamish and Fliss – who I can't imagine life without.

One day maybe you could come over? I know you hate rain, but sometimes it stops, and you should have some fun, Urs, you should fall in love. I wish you would. More than anything, I'd love to see someone adore you.

I wish you would come over. As long as you promise not
to talk about you-know-what.

I love you Urs. I miss . . .

'Can you butter the outside of the toast as well?' A woman
was asking me to make her a toasted cheese sandwich. She was
about eight stone, 40, and her botox made her look like an
escapee from Madame Tussauds. Whenever I saw her, I winced
a little. Scary.

I quickly folded the letter and put it under the desk and went
out the double doors to the kitchen. As I chopped the toast
in half, I overheard Pete talking to the girl sitting in the small
wooden reception booth by the entrance to the steam rooms.

'Why don't you come along?' she asked.

'I'm really not into musicals,' he said.

I popped my head out to see who was chatting him up. It was
a receptionist who was older than me and exceptionally pretty.
She was English, one of the few locals at the Porchester, and she
had never spoken to me. Come to think of it, I'd never spoken to
her either. What would I say? 'What did you do on the weekend?'
'Where are you going this summer?' 'How's your Dad?' It was
terrible, looking back, but I had no interest whatsoever in normality.
I was interested in drinking, smoking, losing the unlosable and in
that huge muscular guy standing by the plant at reception.

Was I?

I could see the girl's reflection in the huge mirror opposite the reception booth. I felt slightly odd about her talking to him like that. How dare she?

'I didn't recognise you with your clothes on,' I said when Pete spotted me peering out from the kitchen.

'I should have threatened to ring the police, then slapped you across the face.'

'What?' This was from the pretty receptionist, quite rightly taken aback by our conversation.

'We just live in the same house.' Pete informed his adoring fan.

'I see you've revived our Aussie native,' Pete said, feeling the wet soil in the pot of the bamboo palm.

'Green fingers,' I said. He smiled and looked at me for too long.

I jumped back inside the kitchen and hit my forehead with my palm. *Green fingers* . . .What a stupid fucking idiot. I peeked out of the kitchen again and watched Pete exit the corner door.

✿

I opened the double doors that led back into the relaxation area. The woman who'd asked for the toasted sandwich wasn't just unhappy about the burnt toast. She was unhappy about the rumours.

'Is it true?' she asked me when I returned with a second attempt. Someone had told her the steam rooms were closing – too expensive, too old fashioned, not enough customers.

'Kate, are we closing?' I checked with the naked mopper.

Her face went white. She rushed to Esther, whose face went similarly white. They'd never worked anywhere else, would never get or manage to hold down a job anywhere else, and both took turns running through the internal door to the swimming pool and gym area to find out if there was any truth to the rumour. There was. The steam rooms were closing soon. Management would do their best to find positions for us in the pool or gym, but things looked pretty grim for the old birds whose skills were limited to the harassment of fresh staff.

I spent the rest of my shift pretending to clean the saunas and steam rooms downstairs. The rooms were in the bowels of the building. You had to walk down the stairs by the plunge pool, past the body-scrub room and the showers then turn the corner before you found them. I sat in one of the small wooden rooms for ages, feeling the badness dripping off my body as I poured water onto the sizzling coals.

After everyone else had gone home, I locked up the steam rooms and pinned the keys I had been entrusted with since my elevation to Employee of the Week to the inside pocket of my polo shirt.

✧

When I got home, the desperate-measure seduction plans I'd made for the evening fell to pieces. Firstly, I had nothing to wear. Fliss had reclaimed much of the gear I'd scavenged since arriving, and all that remained in my room were my grotty jeans and my singlet, and two runners, one of which wasn't mine, and which – on closer inspection – seemed to have a blood stain on it. Secondly, I smelt. No matter how many times I washed, the smell of the squat, particularly my room, seemed to seep into my skin. Thirdly, I hadn't had time to do my nails, and Fliss had stressed that jaggy, unmanicured nails were a sure sign of unpruned bush syndrome, which was apparently enough to put any bloke off. Fourthly, I was starting to realise that having sex with Francesco might be as unappealing as having dinner with him and that there was every chance that he would yell: 'Medium-rare!' when he was ready to be served. And lastly, when I put the runner back down on the floor, I fell over.

I hadn't fainted, just fallen, and this wasn't the first time I'd been a klutz recently: I'd tripped over a non-existent crack in the pavement on the way to work that morning. Now I lay on the floorboards, astonished at my clumsiness. And as I stared at the ceiling, I felt oddly warm, as if I was back in the steam room. I thought I was going insane, but then I smelt smoke. I sniffed at the air, sat up and sniffed, stood up and sniffed, but it seemed to disappear. I knelt down on the floorboards and put my nose to the floor. Definitely smoke. I placed my hand on the floorboards. Definitely warm. I lay down on my stomach and pressed my nose into the crack between the floorboards.

There was smoke coming from the basement.

PART TWO

13

Six feet below, a woman was tied to a chair. The yellow polyester that firmly gagged her mouth was on fire. The woman was Celia. She was thirty-eight and had two children. She'd been in the basement for four weeks.

✿

On the morning she was taken, Celia had finished her single weekly shift, an all-nighter at the hospice off Ladbroke Grove, changed into her power-walking gear, strapped her backpack tight around her back, stopped off at the garage for Walker's salt and vinegar crisps and the latest *Dr Who* magazine, which she'd added to her backpack, and then walked fast for two miles till she reached her street. She'd smiled, excited that she would see the faces of her little boys any moment, that she would climb into the king-size bed the four of them inevitably ended up in and cuddle for at least an hour before the breakfast and school-lunch rush. She was looking forward to waving off the husband she still adored, walking the boys to school, having a second cup of coffee, and then snuggling in bed in front of last night's episode of *The Bill*.

As she passed by the Royal she marvelled at the street she lived in. She and Greg hadn't given in to the suburban pull. They loved the busy, bustling youth of the city, and they never wanted to leave. She often thought such happy thoughts, saying thank you for the luck: for the happy childhood, the well-adjusted sibling, the healthy helpful parents, the job that means something, the husband that still thinks you're the most beautiful woman in the world and regularly tells you so, the groovy flat, the cuddly cat, the children who make you smile and laugh all day, every day.

But Celia didn't get to walk into her flat, or lie in bed with Sam and Johnny, or drink the coffee that Greg would bring in to her at 8 a.m., or make toast and Nutella for breakfast then tuna sandwiches for lunch, or wave goodbye to Greg, or smile and laugh as she walked to school, or watch last night's episode of *The Bill*.

Instead she lost her shoe, and as the flame from her polyester gag began to lick her cheek and catch her hair, she really wished she hadn't.

14

The Sick Man felt very sick. This time it seemed to be concentrated in the stomach area: sharp, stabbing pains. Initially he'd thought of his appendix, forgetting for a second that it had been removed two years earlier. He wondered about his heart, but there were no tingles. He googled several other options, even rang NHS Direct, and was left with the realisation that it must be psychosomatic, a result of the mistake he'd made.

It was a rather big mistake, taking a girl who *belonged*. He thought it would be a relief, but recently, no matter how many ways he did it, he still felt oddly unfulfilled, and was now starting to feel sick into the bargain.

He thought back to when he was ill as a boy. He'd been in bed for five days. Five days alone in the house while his Mum was out somewhere, of sweating and crying and feeling like he wanted to die. On the fifth day he began to feel better, and some time in the afternoon he found himself masturbating. Just as he climaxed he looked out of the window and there she was. A young woman, jogging on the pavement outside his room.

She came to him each time for years, this woman, jogging past him as he pulled, sometimes all of her, sometimes just her face, sometimes only a short white sports sock.

But after a few years she faded, and he had to get help to find her again. In the park maybe? The sports shop? Sluttysporty.com? Images of trim healthiness returned at each window-shopping expedition and he lay in bed feeling better momentarily, just as he had when she'd jogged outside his twelve-year-old self's bedroom window.

It was after he moved to London he realised the window-shopping had stopped working; like a relationship gone stale, it was no longer enough. After weeks of failed attempts to climax, he decided he would need to do more than browse. He would need to make a purchase.

✧

He knew her, had even smiled at her a couple of times. Knew where she lived, what she liked for lunch, that on Tuesday mornings she got home at around 5.15 a.m.

He'd watched her do the same thing for two Tuesdays in a row, and had tried the old way many times, the battered curtain his mask, but he could never quite get there, so on the third Tuesday he implemented the plan he had rehearsed: At 5.15 a.m. the girl would walk, smiling, down the hill and past the hostel. She would bleed a little after the blow to the back of the head. She would be none the wiser as he dragged her from the pavement and into the abandoned house. None the wiser as he carried her through the abandoned hall, down the staircase into the basement.

That's where it ended, the plan, and it had gone perfectly well at first, but after that, he'd had to make it up as he went along.

She woke up earlier than he expected, but he was ready. He was wearing his chosen face – a gimp mask – jeans and an old T-shirt. His mouth seemed to gleam through the custom-made holes in the taut, shiny black leather. Big eyes stared at her. Huge eyes, opposite her, in the corner of the room. Gagged and tied to her chair, she woke. He watched her face as the fear swept over it. Her eyes wide and white. Her forehead deeply lined from the pressure of silent yells. Her mouth dribbling. Legs red-raw with wriggling, rubbing, trying, begging.

A few hours later he touched her gently on the side of the head. She was less rigid and the cries had moved downwards to pound in her stomach. He took to his seat again, nervous that after all the effort it wouldn't work. He took a few breaths, in and out, slowly in and out, and then unzipped his trousers. Watching her eyes widen again, he took his soft penis in his hand and held it. Then he began. Slowly . . . make it good . . . . this is it . . . up and down, concentrate, nearly there, nearly there. She was wriggling, and he liked that. He focused on her legs, clad in Lycra and ankle socks and he noticed for the first time that she only had one shoe. Fuck.

He zipped himself up, ran up the staircase, opened the door to the hall, tripped on a floorboard, picked himself up in a frenzy, fumbled with the front door-handle, and walked onto the street. He searched awkwardly in the new daylight for the evidence, bent down and looked under a car, banging his head on the way back up, and finally – thank God – found the shoe under the metallic blue Honda Jazz that was parked ten feet from the front door. He picked up the shoe and checked the street until he felt confident that he hadn't forgotten anything else. He was about to return to the task at hand when he noticed someone walking towards the Kensington Gardens end of the street. He panicked, tossing the trainer into the bin beside him, then went back inside.

He was a little annoyed after the whole shoe incident, so when he got into the basement room he didn't even sit in his chair. He unzipped again, knelt beside the shoeless foot, the toes wriggling a protest against his left hand's strokes, and tugged twice, unbelievably, just twice, before it happened. Ah, he said, opening his eyes. Ah, ah, he said, licking his achievement from the sock-clad foot.

15

When she'd woken, Celia had assumed it was a dream. Like the one where she'd forgotten to feed Johnny, where he'd become so thin and boggly-eyed that she'd screamed in horror and thrown him against the wall. Or the one where she'd slept with Greg's best friend and he'd found out and left her. But she didn't wake up, didn't roll over to her husband to say: 'Greg, I had a bad dream, do you still love me?' Or to her little boys, to say: 'Good morning, my beautiful little boys! Are you hungry?' But she couldn't move her hands to slap or pinch herself, and no matter how hard she looked the boys weren't there, the bed wasn't there, Greg wasn't there, and it came to her that this was real. She was in a dark room. Her trousers and pants had been pulled down to her knees. There was a hole in her chair and a bucket underneath it. She was tied and gagged.

She'd never imagined coping in such a scenario, so she had nothing to draw on. No inner resources to help with the first few hours, where she'd tried her hardest to get a noise from the inside of her to the out, all the while a masked man three feet from her, watching, just watching. The noise didn't come. It got stuck somewhere in her throat, dribbles of it dampening the material that dug deep around her mouth. She didn't give up as such, but after hours of internal screaming, of banging and rubbing against the ties, she rested, just for a moment, to gather her strength. He smiled at her as she drooled, poised like a rabid dog with mouth guard and chain.

◇

It was a long time before the people moved in above her. During this time, she'd made a rule that she must concentrate on survival and not on him, what he did to her. So each time after he left she pressed her chin to the locket round her neck – a silver heart-shaped locket on a chain, with a picture of her family inside. She touched it with her chin for strength and luck, and then resumed her projects with focus and determination.

She was tied to a chair in the middle of the small, square, low-ceilinged windowless room. A plastic-coated bicycle chain was looped through one of the slats on the back of the chair and then padlocked tightly to a metal ring that was bolted to the floor. Her hands were bound together behind her back. Each foot was tied to a chair leg. Thick rope was wound around and around her legs and torso. A polyester bandanna tore into her mouth. A lamp, which he always turned off when he was finished, sat on a metal table in the corner. There was a small grate at the top of the right wall. A bucket of her by-products was under her chair. Just outside the room, she'd caught glimpse of a staircase that led to the real world. She didn't know what world it was. It could have been Bulgaria for all she knew.

She decided the only way to loosen the rope was to wriggle fingers, toes, feet, to rub and squirm and move as much as she could. She did this for hours each day, first the hands, then the feet, then the whole body. Wriggle and rest. Wriggle and rest.

She peppered this plan with others, so as to not lose motivation. The gag. Get it off, and yell. She pressed her head against her shoulder and rubbed. She bit and chewed at the polyester.

She rocked the chair. Back and forth, side to side, to try and move it, loosen the bicycle chain. But the chain was securely locked.

She tried to bang the chair on the ground, lift the front two legs, bang it down. Make a noise. The noise it made was tiny, pathetic, and she came so close to making the chair fall over that it panicked her. If she fell over, she decided, she would be in an even worse position.

In those first terrible weeks, Celia's concerted efforts had not paid off. Her ropes were still secure, her gag unloosened, and her chair in the same position.

'You've not been washing, have you? You're a smelly girl,' he'd said during one of his twilight visits. 'We'll have to think about a bath.'

After the bath comment, Celia spent hours stretching her feet towards the bucket underneath the hole in her chair. It happened during her third shift, as she'd taken to calling her long impassioned efforts. The bucket swished onto her feet and all over the floor. She then rocked and rocked so hard that her chair fell to the ground with a bang. It knocked her out, but when she woke she smiled underneath her gag, because it had worked. She was swimming in her own waste, would marinate in it for days, and now she would definitely be in need of a bath.

16

Fuck, he hadn't meant to do that.

He'd come in after his trip to the all-night Asda and found himself doing something he hadn't meant to do.

For a week it had been excellent.

He'd visited her each night at the same time. He would get impatient as the working day drew to a close, excitement pumping through him. He found the normal evening tasks almost impossible to bear as he waited for the right time to enter the basement. He went in through the back garden, climbing over the high wall, creeping across the small patch of grass, opening the kitchen door, walking into the hall, and then opening the cupboard. It had a lock and a door at the back that was hidden by wallpaper and piled up cans of paint. He had put padlocks on this inner door, and made sure to pile the paint high each time he left, just in case. Beyond the second door was an old wooden staircase that went down to the basement. There were two rooms off the small, concreted hall, one locked, one without a door.

Despite his clumsiness, the first night had been the best, crawling through the garden, opening door after door after door, then finding her just as he'd left her that morning, a parent seeing a newborn baby waking for the first time. He smiled as her eyes opened wide, very wide. His girl, still fresh, in white socks and trainers, Lycra trousers. Fit and feisty and . . . he kissed her on the cheek and on the nose. He licked her left ear, then under her right. He put his tongue in her right ear, as far as he could, then swept it across her forehead, tasting the salt of her fear. She sat still, her eyes closed now, tightly, as he rubbed himself around her face until the 'Ah' meant that it was all over, all over her chin.

Seven nights in a row. *Ah, nearly there, nearly there*, then he'd take her gag off, put a knife to her throat to stop her yelling – although he wasn't too worried, really, no one would hear. He'd feed her with a spoon, water her with a straw, chat about the day's events, put the gag back on, the light out, then leave through door after door after door to the real world again.

In the second week the smell of the bucket really began to make him queasy and he decided to come every second day. She remained in the chair, and he wondered how she had managed to get into such a state, just sitting there.

Only one visit in the third week. He'd been busy and when he came back to see her it was less than excellent. She'd spilt the bucket and her chair was lying sideways on the ground in a puddle of shit and piss. He gagged. She'd let herself go, needed to take better care, so he made a deal with her as he placed the chair upright: 'I'll untie you if you're a good girl. No yelling, no trying anything, I just need to clean you up.'

She'd nodded with her once-pretty face, and he unlocked the padlock that secured the chair to the metal ring on the floor. He picked up the chair and placed her on it. He then carried her and her chair away from the wet brown stench. He took off her bandanna. Her mouth stayed in the same position for a while, as if the cloth was still there, but eventually he saw the face that had appealed to him on the street. The dark brown eyes, the straight black hair, the optimum weight and height, health and muscle and freshness and fitness.

He put his finger over her mouth and she obeyed, remaining silent as he untied her for the sponge bath.

He wiped her left arm first. The trickle as he squeezed the dirtied water into the basin made a sound that reminded him of when he'd been ill, and his Mum had cooled his forehead.

He held each of her hands gently as he cleaned to the elbow, and then he pulled her T-shirt up above her breasts. He unclipped her bra and cleaned each breast with the soapy sponge. He took her hands and helped her hold them up so the T-shirt could be taken off. He helped her stand so that he could take off her Lycra track-pants and socks and wipe the parts that had been naked since that first day, when he'd kindly pulled everything down to the knees. He put her clothing in a black bin bag and wiped slowly – up, around – then wiped the seat that he had carved a hole in before she'd arrived. He guided her back to her sitting position. He wiped her face and eyes with the sponge and then he bent down to wash her feet.

And that's when it happened. After he pressed the wet sponge between her big toe and the one next to it, she kicked him. He fell to the floor. His nose was bleeding. He watched for a moment as she ran out of the room and towards the stairs. She clambered up one, two, three, four steps. He stood up as she fumbled with one of the inner locks he was always careful to secure after entering the hidden door. She bashed at the padlock and chain with her hand, over and over, as if this would break it. She held the door handle and pulled at it, yelling HELP. He stood up, walked up the stairs slowly, towards her naked, banging, yelling body. She turned around and faced him.

He smashed her in the right cheek with his fist. She fell down the stairs, her naked limbs bumping until they landed untidily at the bottom. He walked back down the stairs and kicked her before she had a chance to get up. Then he kicked her again. And again. He couldn't stop his foot from booting her in the side, in the leg, and then in the head. It was an oversized foot-tick, unstoppable, and he fell to the floor beside her, exhausted, when it finally stalled.

He opened his eyes at the same time she did. Fuck, he hadn't meant to do that. She was now not only stinking and filthy, but also cut and swollen. Her muscular legs were covered in blood and, from several angles, even looked flabby. One of her finger bones was sticking out of its skin. Her face was barely a face, her back bony and bruised.

He tied her limp, naked body to the chair, the blood from his nose dripping onto her stomach and legs. He could hardly look at her. She was disgusting. A favourite porn vid gone fuzzy.

◇

When he left the basement room with a bin bag of shitty clothing, he hadn't fed her with a spoon and watered her with a straw, hadn't gone over the events of the day, hadn't placed the bucket under her scrawny arse or chained the chair to the metal ring in the middle of the room. He hadn't even tied the ropes very well.

As he quickly concealed the secret door with cans of magnolia eggshell and matt, he wondered if he would have the stomach to visit her again.

◇

Bayswater was turning out to be the perfect place – vigorous youth all round, in the hostels, the bars, the park, the leisure centre down the road. He was so excited by what was on offer that he almost managed to forget all about this last mistake, this thing who had a life and people who were looking for her.

He could do that, couldn't he? Ignore the sick feeling, drown it with a glass of cider? Start over again, with that one in the netball skirt perhaps?

Then one evening, after walking back from the park, he noticed someone fiddling about at the doorway. He watched from behind a tree as the girls ran inside giggling. Shit. They'd gone in. He watched as they went out again, then carried mattresses and junk back in through the front door. Shit. He felt desperately ill. They'd moved into the house. He took stock. She was underneath. The cupboard was locked and the door well disguised.

But shit. The place had been empty for months, and they had to pick *now* to take it over. He gulped nervously as he watched, wondering what it meant for him. Could he stop them? What could he do? He was always so careful, so thorough, and this was a terrible snag. He would have to sort it out, that much was for sure. The question was: *How?*

17

Celia woke when she heard the footsteps. Light and darkness had come and gone. Terror, pain, boredom and anger had consumed the slow minutes. He'd not visited for a long time, she wasn't sure how long, but it was long enough to allow her to move more than she'd managed before. She'd been beaten badly and had a fractured finger and cuts and bruises all over, but she kept her focus – think about escape, nothing else. In his anger and frustration at her attempt to run away, he'd done a poor job of tying her up. While her gag was as secure as before, her hands were in front of her now, tied together but not to the chair, and her legs felt a little looser. Most importantly, the chair was no longer chained to the metal ring in the middle of the room and could be moved an inch at a time if she zigzagged carefully.

Her first expedition was to the drainpipe adjacent to the grate. The pipe was leaking a bit and she desperately needed water. She'd learned at college about dehydration and starvation, and knew how long she had: about twenty days without food, three or four without water. She was naked except for her necklace. Her gag was still secure, and it was driving her crazy. The lack of water had made her lips crack, her tongue swell, and she felt like vomiting. She knew if she did vomit she would die, choke on it and die, so she moved inch by inch over to the drainpipe and held her mouth against the dripping metal. It took almost an hour to soak the gag, but eventually it was sodden and she sighed with relief as she sucked the cloth to wet her mouth. She had bought herself some time.

Her second expedition was to get out of the room and into the small hall. The room she'd been trapped in didn't have a door, but a piece of wood was still hammered into the ground where the door once was, and it took about four attempts before she managed to bump the chair legs over it.

The hall was about five feet square, with a staircase at one end, her doorless room to the right of it, and a locked door to the left. She couldn't get up the stairs in her chair, or into the second room, and otherwise the hall was completely empty. The expedition proved fruitless and the hall stank even more than her shit, so she moved back into the room she now thought of as *her* room.

Her next project was to saw through her hand ties using the corner of the metal table that had the lamp on it. She was making her way towards the table when she heard the noise upstairs. Assuming it was him, she straightened herself and looked back towards the staircase. Funny, she almost wanted to see him. He might take the gag off to feed and water her, like in the good old days.

But he didn't come down the stairs. And the footsteps got louder. And there was more than one set of them. There was laughter, squealing, the moving of furniture.

A frenzy of activity overtook her. A party was going on somewhere in the house – there were many voices, loud music. She rocked the chair from side to side, banged her head against the drainpipe, moved over to the table and pushed it with her chair to make a loud scraping noise. But the party upstairs was so loud that no one could hear her. She banged her head against the wall . . . and knocked herself out.

When she woke it was light and quiet. She cried waterless tears. Her focus was weakening. She slept.

It was dark again and the voices were muffled and distant. She soaked and sucked from her gag and waited for the right moment. She could hear someone entering the room above her, moving around, going quiet, talking to herself, alone. It had to be her bedroom.

Celia scraped her chair along the ground. Then she scraped it back again. She could hear someone getting up, walking across the floorboards directly above her head. Celia followed the shuddering boards with her desperate eyes. A door above creaked open. Feet left the room; floorboards stopped shuddering. Celia's eyes flickered from side to side. Where had they gone? Had they heard? Were they coming down to save her?

The footsteps returned to the room and it went quiet again. She hadn't heard.

Celia realised she would have to redouble her efforts. She rocked her chair from front to back, again and again, and after three or four hefty sways, the chair toppled forwards with a loud bang.

With her forehead bleeding onto the ground, Celia listened. Had the girl heard this time?

She had heard! She was getting up, walking over to the door, saying something. Celia held her breath and waited. A man's voice. The girl's voice. Then silence. Silence.

All night.

It hadn't worked. Not only that, but now she was on the

floor and no matter how hard she tried, it was impossible to move.

Celia lay in that position for two days.

18

It wasn't so hard in the end. Just had to keep an eye on the place, wait for the familiar faces to get out of the way for a while, or at least out of hearing distance, then go in, just as before. He was surprised how easy it was. The residents were noisy dope smokers, stoned and/or pissed most of the time. Their hygiene was, on the whole, pretty poor, so no one seemed to have heard or smelt anything. No one had the foggiest.

The hardest thing was finding the motivation and he only managed because he realised it would be easier to get her out sooner rather than later. She could go the way he did, walking, and he could take her somewhere else then think about what to do.

When he arrived he was angry with her. For getting as bad as this. She was on the floor again, stinking and bleeding all over.

'Fucking hell!' he'd snarled as quietly as he could after he turned on the light.

He kicked her, untied her till she flopped into a silent brown puddle on the ground, then slowly poured over her the bucket of water he'd brought with him. He towelled her down until she looked something like a woman again.

He'd never been very good in bed, never quite knew how to get it going, and he wondered if anger might do the job. He was furious.

But he wasn't sure how to position himself. At first he laid her spread-eagled on her back on the ground. Her eyes were open but dead-looking, her mouth still gagged. She closed her eyes when he told her to, and then he undressed and lay on top of her for some time before realising that this just wasn't going to work. He needed to get the anger back.

He made her stand up. 'Fight me!' he said.

She did as she was told, slapping him on the chest, without conviction.

He punched her in the face and told her to do it again, which she did. She hit him twice, with conviction. He turned her around, made her put her hands on the back of the chair and spread her legs, but it still didn't work.

He sat on the chair and asked her to straddle him.

No good.

Against the wall, two hands on her throat. This made her struggle and wriggle, which made him angrier and angrier. He pushed up into her.

✿

'Oh God, you're a lazy cow!' he'd said afterwards, throwing her to the ground. He was revolted by the whole thing, so much so that he decided to put off taking her out. He rushed to get out of there, away from the repulsive stink. He tied her as quickly as he could, crept up the stairs, opened the hidden cupboard door, quietly locked and concealed it with the paint and wallpaper, and crept out into the hallway.

19

As much as Celia had hated it, the rape had seemed almost irrelevant. She'd long lost possession of her body, had separated her mind from it, so when he'd managed the hardness and lifted her against the wall to thrust while panting into her nose, she'd hardly flinched. This was not her. She was somewhere else altogether.

And on the bright side, the fucking had made him sloppy. While his knots were as neat and professional as before, he'd tied her hands together less tightly, and in front of her again. He hadn't padlocked the chair to the floor. He'd tied her feet less securely, so she could wriggle them wildly and zigzag the chair freely. As for the rope around her torso, it was pathetic. There was about an inch of movement between her back and the back of the chair.

After he'd crept back upstairs, a positive feeling overwhelmed her. With moving fingers, wriggling toes, a padlock, and a bicycle chain, the world was her oyster.

✧

Celia split the days into sections. On her first shift she rubbed the ropes in the hope of weakening them. They were about a quarter of an inch thick, made of white nylon . . . and unyielding. Celia rubbed as much as she could with her hands and legs, pressing against wall, chair, pipe, table, but the knots were steadfast, and the ropes appeared to be completely resistant to abrasion and stretching.

Her second shift involved trying to climb the stairs while still in her chair. She positioned herself at the bottom step and knocked herself forwards so that her chin landed on the third step. She then tried to get her knees onto the first step in order to edge her way upwards, using chin and knees, one step at a time. In the end, getting out of that initial position became her primary goal, because the plan was a hopeless one.

During the third shift she banged at the walls with her fists and if her fists got too sore she used her forehead hoping that someone, anyone, would hear – one of the new residents upstairs, a passer-by perhaps, someone taking the rubbish out, a neighbour getting storage from the adjacent basement . . . anyone.

The fourth shift she used the padlock to chip around the lock of the door in the hall.

Her fifth: she used the padlock arch to pull at her ropes and gag.

Sixth: bang the bicycle chain against the floor.

Seven, suck at the wet gag.

But her rope ties and her mouth gag would not budge, the

locked door would not open, the stairs were insurmountable and there seemed to be no one within hearing distance, no one listening.

○

Celia had always been a determined person. She'd walked before her fellow nursery babies had. She'd refused the bottle till she was two. She'd never eaten cauliflower. And the births of both boys had been homers, agonising, drug-free, in-the-bath homers. She never gave up on anything – not when Greg said he wasn't sure about having kids, or when Johnny refused to say thank you, or when Sam declared that he never wanted to ride a bike anyway, ever. Throughout her life, Celia had achieved all the goals she set herself.

But after weeks of keeping her goal-achieving head on, despite the worst, most awful scenario imaginable, Celia was beginning to realise that on this occasion, she would have to give up.

It had been about ten nights since the people moved in above – she didn't know exactly how long, because at least one of the changes from light to dark had eluded her – and she had tried everything. She'd used all her mental energy, all her physical reserves, and was now realising that it was time to surrender. She would die. She would never see Greg or Johnny or Sam again. They would never find her body, never know that she had been kidnapped just outside their house, then taken away, beaten, raped and starved. It would be better to die, she thought, as she sat in her chair at the foot of the staircase.

She was in the stinking hall again when she heard a tap running. There must be a bathroom beside the girl's bedroom, she thought to herself. She followed the noise down the wall where it swished down through a pipe. She moved over to the pipe and banged at it with her hands. Good solid bangs that she was proud of. She kept going until she heard a noise from the bathroom – the girl again. A noise and then feet and then silence. Celia moved her chair towards the bicycle chain in the main room. She could use this to make a louder noise. She had almost reached it when the footsteps returned and Celia heard water gushing down the pipe. The girl was emptying the bath, and Celia was in the wrong position to bang at the pipe. By the time she'd zigzagged back over, the girl had gone.

For a long time, Celia bashed at the pipe with her chain. Its echo gave her a better chance, she figured. But nothing came of it except more blood from her shredded hands.

⋄

Hours later, in her chair-prison, Celia lowered her head to begin dying. She may as well do it there. Why move? Why do anything?

Meow.

Maybe this was heaven, Celia thought.

Meow.

Bobby was going to greet her in heaven. Maybe the boys would be there too?

Meow.

She opened her eyes. She was still in hell.

Meow.

Bobby was in hell?

'Bobby?' She looked around the square hallway – there it was again. She followed the noise as fast as she could, moving a couple of inches at a time before getting back into *her* room.

Bobby was meowing at the grate. Oh God, Bobby.

She edged her way over to the wall and looked up at her cat. He'd found her. How? As she stared into his eyes, she reasoned that she mustn't be very far from home.

The grate was about a foot wide and ten inches high. A couple of the metal slats were missing, and Bobby was able to stick his head in. But he couldn't squeeze the rest of himself through, as much as he seemed to want to. He kept meowing at Celia, pushing himself this way and that.

Come on Bobs, come on, she thought to herself, stretching her tied hands as far as she could until they were less than a foot from his head.

He seemed to stop. Was he stuck? She hoped he was, and that he would meow so loudly that a neighbour would hear. '*Meow*! Bobby, meow!' she tried to say with her eyes. Someone might come and find you, find me.

But he didn't meow and he wasn't stuck. He was performing

103

cat magic, manipulating his body without seeming to move, then plunging down to her feet with a whoosh. Two slats from the grate fell, one of them onto Celia's lap, which she clutched with a new-found instinct to gather tools and weapons. The second slat missed Bobby by an inch and landed on the floor as he jumped up to her.

Celia touched him, bent down to feel him with her face. She scoured the room, thinking hard, breathing loudly through her nose, and then it came to her. Her locket – a silver heart with an unreachable photo of her boys inside. It wasn't so hard to take it off now that her hands were in front of her, and she could wriggle her fingers a little. She wondered why she'd not thought of a use for it earlier. Although, she thought fleetingly, she would probably have used it to try and kill herself, and she was glad now that she hadn't.

She placed the silver chain and heart-shaped locket around Bobby's neck. She then lifted him as high as she could in her tied, twisted hands. He pounced a foot into the air, meowing loudly and clearing the opening easily now that all but one of the metal slats were missing. He ran off with his message.

She couldn't believe her luck. Bobby would take the locket home and they would follow him back, just like Lassie.

✿

Distant sirens fizzled with her heartbeat. Voices wafted through the grate and out again, a bark and a wheelie bin lid, footsteps, taps and doors. It was an award-winning solution, and she had been elated for some time, but as the voices and the sounds of the doors faded, she realised that Bobby was just a damn cat, not a particularly cunning one at that, who had probably dropped the locket in the back lane and then skulked off to lick himself somewhere. She found some voice in her throat to moan and she lowered her head to look for comfort in it.

A song. Celia stopped the moan, lifted her head, and listened. A Beatles number, with the perfect lyrics coming from above the grate. She zigzagged until she was directly underneath the music and reached with the metal slat that had fallen into her lap as high as she could in order to jab at the low ceiling. She stretched and stretched herself until the one-foot piece of metal was a quarter of an inch from the roof. She couldn't reach. She tried to make the chair jump but each time she did, the metal slat in her outstretched hand failed to make contact. Fuck, she thought, holding the slat as tightly as she could. The girl was playing the song for the fourth time. She would stop soon, surely. She had to make this one work. She steadied herself, stretched her hand, and jumped.

Help me!

She'd made contact! The chair thumped back to the floor.

Help me!

20

She'd honestly expected the footsteps to be the police. It was still light. He never came when it was light. This had to be the police, or the girl, at last. But why were they being so careful? Why were seventeen cars not screeching to a halt around the building, their contents spilling out, surrounding, taking aim, storming, then saving her?

It wasn't the police. It was him. He had Bobby in his arms. 'Very creative,' he said, toying with the necklace.

Bobby hissed and lashed at his captor's hand.

'Ow!' said the masked man, throwing the cat down and nursing his scratched wrist. Bobby immediately rushed over to his owner, and curled into her naked lap. Celia moaned as she put her hands on him, more so as the man approached and snatched the cat from her. Celia reached with her tied hands to stop him. The cat screeched, desperate to get away. Kneeling on the floor, the man held Bobby between his knees, while roughly knotting the locket-chain around his neck. He smiled at Celia's pleading eyes, then stood up with Bobby in his hands. He lifted the cat high . . . and let go. Bobby wriggled as the noose strangled him, his paws dangling just an inch from the floor. The man waited for the movement to subside, as if holding a spinning yo-yo. Afterwards, just to make a point, the man pulled at the chain-knot until the cat's head severed and flopped onto the ground.

✧

It was getting tiresome. He would have to kill her now. This was annoying because killing wasn't particularly his thing, but she was in no state to go out alive and she'd heard him speak too much, knew his voice. He could do it and leave her with the others. If no one had found them yet, no one ever would. But he had somewhere to go. In fact, he was late.

'I'm going to kill you tomorrow,' he said, leaving Celia and the pieces of her cat in their joint grave.

When he left, he forgot to turn off the light.

21

Oh God. She shut her eyes tightly and turned from the decapitated cat, staying in that position till it was dark outside, not looking, not moving. Eventually she noticed that a light was shining in her eyes. And it was smelly. She squinted at the bulb in the corner of the room. The light was white and sharp. Too strong . . . 100 watts – her eyes had adjusted and she could now read it on the bulb. The inner white lining of the orange lampshade was being tinged brown from the heat.

She moved over to the lampshade. The edges of the bandanna that gagged her mouth were loose and flimsy, the perfect kindling. She began heating the loose ends. Steam rose from the evaporating drain water. Bending over the hot bulb, the polyester warmed itself and before long it was smoking. Her intention was to weaken the material, burn a bit of it, so that it might come undone, but when it began smoking she realised it could also act as a signal. She moved her head from side to side, giving oxygen, making the smoke rise, and soon the room was thick with smoke . . . and her hair was on fire.

She yelled through the flaming cloth and banged her head against her shoulder and then against the lamp, which smashed to pieces on the floor, and then against the wall until the fire was out. She smouldered for a few seconds, before realising that this, her last and most horrific project, had not worked. Not only that, it had burnt the hair from her head, and some of the skin from her face.

As the endorphins raced to her injuries, Celia realised that this was the end. She nodded to herself – she would finish herself off before he arrived to kill her. She wouldn't give him the satisfaction of doing it. It would be on her terms. She scoured the room for tools – the smashed and useless lamp, the metal table, the locket, the bicycle chain, the dead cat, the metal slats that had fallen from the grate, the bucket, the chair, the table, the drainpipe. There were many options – broken lamp to wrists, bicycle chain to neck. In the end she decided she would do what her uncle Mark had done with his unwanted puppies. She would smash her head against the wall. This way, at least, she would be expressing exactly how she felt about having to kill herself . . . Because in truth, it really fucking pissed her off.

She would begin the following day. Until then, she would give herself a wake. She would reflect on her mostly blessed life, think about her Mum and her Dad, her big brother, about Johnny's curly hair and Sam's perfect grammar and neat handwriting, about the conversation she and Greg would often have, which always started with him asking:

Who loves you?

You do.

Why?

Because I'm lovable.

Why?

Because God made me that way.

PART THREE

22

It stopped. By the time Fliss had responded to my scream of 'Fire!' and raced into my room, the smoke had disappeared. Like magic.

'Must have been our bong, or someone having a barbecue,' Fliss said. I sniffed the air again, sniffed the boards, but there was no trace of smoke *or* heat. Jesus Christ, I needed to do more than stop taking drugs. I needed a psychiatrist.

'You don't need a psychiatrist,' Fliss said, sitting on the boards beside me and popping one of her magic pills into my mouth. 'You just need to get dressed.'

I looked where she was looking. Shit, I was naked. I had been lying naked before another human being for minutes, sprawled face down on the floor, sniffing and groping at the boards with my hands like some barenaked madwoman.

'Sexual Lesson number 34b,' Fliss said, '. . . and this is very, very important . . .'

I had covered myself with the sleeping bag, and was listening carefully, although in truth Fliss's sexual lessons had proved bloody useless thus far.

'Is to never, ever . . . stink of shit.'

I was gobsmacked. Did I really stink of shit? Why had no one said anything? 'The burning smell's a welcome change,' Fliss said, opening my window and spraying some perfume into the air. She told me the smell from my room seemed to have seeped out into the hallway and that I should think about giving up peanut butter. She also said that I lacked conviction.

'All a girl needs to do is *decide* she wants sex, then have it. Simple. Do you want to?'

'Yes.'

'Then pick someone, and do it, tonight.'

'Okay,' I said, before scrubbing myself so hard in the shower that I almost bled. Before heading out, I sprayed my room with Fliss's perfume again and threw out the catering size tub of crunchy peanut butter that Hamish had given me.

○

An hour later, a bunch of us shared a taxi to Club Wolf. As the black cab motored along Ladbroke Grove, I began to forget the goings-on in the house and smile at the London sights that whizzed by – the people of different colours, different styles, walking fast along busy streets. I loved London. I loved everyone in the taxi, and the neat queue at the door of the club, the music inside, the way Cheryl-Anne grinned widely as she danced even though she had a child who was 12,000 miles away and even though she had used the phrase: 'Those bloody Abos' on more than one occasion. I loved how Fliss nabbed a man who wasn't Zach ten seconds after arriving. How Zach didn't seem to give a shit. And I loved my men – all three of whom danced with me for hours: Pete, self-conscious and awkward, thinking about each step and oft-times pointing; Francesco, groovy and outlandish, dancing with me but *not* with me; and Hamish, cute and comfortable, at home with the beat, always smiling. Although I had planned to lose my virginity to Francesco and Francesco alone, the lights and the music spoke to me clear as day. I could lose my virginity to any one of these men, because at 12 o'clock, when the dancing ended, I loved each of them just the same.

✧

It was time to huddle in a quiet club corner and look at each other. Cheryl-Anne had tried it on with Pete some time earlier. 'I think he's retarded,' she'd announced after several raunchy dances and an actual quad lick. He'd pulled her up from her licking position and asked if she would like a glass of water. When she said no, he said: 'Well, I do. Could you get it for me?' Cheryl-Anne flicked her hair and set about finding a set of biceps that would appreciate the acrobatics of her tongue. Zach ended up on stage with someone else's guitar. Fliss snogged three men then took one of them outside for a walk.

'What time is it?' I asked Francesco, whose forehead seemed very shiny. 'Midnight,' he said, 'Can you believe it?'

I didn't answer him. Didn't need to. We all knew that it was unbelievable and amazing for the time to actually be midnight.

'What's the time?' I asked Francesco a moment later.

'Midnight,' he said.

'Wow.'

'You guys are fucked,' said Pete from his non-drug-taking position of superiority.

The staring turned to touching when Francesco stroked my face. I loved Francesco. When I reciprocated the stroke, I noticed his face was moist. Pete's felt rougher, manly. Hamish's was a bit weird . . . like polystyrene. Apparently my face was soft and beautiful. All of them agreed on this.

We took turns ordering drinks. Francesco ordered real champagne. Hamish ordered vodka and lemonade. I ordered red wine and tonic with a splash of Bailey's for colour and texture. Pete ordered water. Apparently my concoction was the worst drink any of them had ever had.

❖

'I'm a virgin,' I said as the four of us taxied home. 'I've been trying to give it to Francesco but he won't take it and his option is running out.' My head was out the window. London was rushing through my hair. I brought my head back inside the taxi and looked at my boys.

'Why won't you fuck me, Francesco?

'I'm a slut.'

'But that's perfect!'

'I'm in slut mode. Wham. Bam. Piss off. I accidentally got to know you. I don't fuck people I know . . . God, too much responsibility.'

'So have you been with anyone since we met?'

'Let me think . . . yes.'

'No!'

'Most nights.'

'No!'

'Yes.'

'I'm so dumb. Fliss says I'm dumb. Fliss says I need to wake up and wear more makeup, which could be a song. Fliss says all I need to do is pick someone, then just do it with them, just like that, 'cause I'm a girl. So . . . what about you, Hamish? . . . or Pete . . . *and* Pete . . . and Francesco. Oh, I can't choose! I know, I'll find a place to put each one of you!'

'Shut up,' Pete said.

'I just want to have a fuck.'

'If you don't shut up I'll ask the driver to stop.'

'What's wrong with you boys? I'm offering a hymen-breaking eardrum-rupturing group fuck!'

Pete asked the driver to stop, opened the door, shoved me out of the car, and then shut it again. The other two boys seemed to be giggling as I stood open-mouthed on the side of the road. I was in the same position when the car stopped fifty

116

metres ahead to let Pete out. He walked towards me and the taxi took off again.

'What is wrong with you?' I screamed as he approached me.

'You're completely mashed, Bronwyn. You don't know what you're talking about.'

'Fuck you.'

'You just offered yourself to three men, at the same time.'

'So?'

'So stop saying the word fuck.'

I began walking along the dark, littered street as fast as I could, muttering the 'f' word over and over till it made no sense. The wave had gone, for now, and I didn't love everything so much. Bastard, humiliating me like that, ruining my night. He walked two steps behind me and no matter how fast I walked, I couldn't lose him. After three blocks, I stopped and turned suddenly.

'Why won't anyone take my virginity? Am I ugly?'

Pete stopped. 'No.'

'I'm stupid then.'

'Francesco likes it kinky – in public. He told me that last night he did it in the Ladies' at Whiteley's Shopping Centre with some girl from the kebab shop. After that public kiss in the squat, he probably realised you wouldn't go for that.'

'I *am* stupid.'

'Sometimes, but mostly sad. I think you're trying to be happy, but I'm not sure it's working. What's going on inside that head?'

'Nothing.'

'Have you done something you're ashamed of?'

'Why? No.'

'Is there something that terrifies you?'

'No!'

'You've been stoned since you got here. You've seen nothing. You've done nothing.'

'I went to Oxford.'

'You went to a pub.'

'Bugger off.'

'Why are you holding back? What are you scared of? Who are you?'

'Who are *you*, Mr Pete?' I asked. The wave had returned, that swimming, lovey feeling the second pill gave.

'I'm Peter McGuire, I'm 24 and I'm from a town outside of Adelaide. My mother's a drunk. My father's English. I'm in love with you.'

'I'm in love with you too,' I said, stroking his rough face.

'No, not drug-induced. I feel like you're my home.'

'Oh! I think you're a home too.'

'Jesus Christ!' Pete was annoyed at me for some reason, maybe because as I said the thing about a home I fell over. He walked off in a huff, the weirdo, and after picking myself up I ended up following his rigid square shoulders as they punched at the night.

23

At 2 a.m., all three boys were still awake. Bobby hadn't come home, and the household was no longer flippant about late arrivals.

It was five weeks since *that* Tuesday, when Johnny and Sam had woken to the sound of their Dad's alarm. Radio 2 it was, cheerful and unimposing. They'd looked across at each other from their parents' super king-size bed, which is where the boys always ended up.

'Where is she?' Johnny had asked. He'd woken and stretched out to find her, but she wasn't there. Wasn't in the middle of them, warm and smiling, for the morning cuddle after working all night to get them toys and holidays.

'Where is she?' Johnny had yelled to his Dad, who was brewing the coffee.

'What?'

'Mummy? She's not here.'

'I can't hear you.'

'Mummy's not here.'

'Don't yell,' Greg had said, two coffees in his hand. 'I think she's in the loo.'

Greg put the coffees on the table beside the bed.

'Ceils!' he'd said lovingly, knocking on the door of the toilet.

'Ceils!' he'd said lovingly, peering into the study.

'Ceils!' he'd said lovingly, checking out the boys' room and the living room.

'Ceils!' he'd said, doing all of the above, again.

'Celia!' he'd said to her voicemail.

'CELIA!' into the street after he'd phoned work.

Into Kensington Gardens after he'd phoned the police.

The tube.

Whiteley's Shopping Centre.

Her Mum's.

Her good friends.

Her not-so-good friends.

Kensington Gardens again.

'CELIA, CELIA, CELIA!'

✿

Hell was not knowing. Greg had experienced the feeling in miniature – waiting for Celia to say yes, she would marry him; for the doctor to say no, the foetus did not have Down's Syndrome. But not knowing where she was, what she was doing, if she was alive – this level of not knowing was hot, burning, crazy hell.

He could split it into sections, how it had eaten him alive. First was that strange calm. It felt like when Sam was three and had disappeared in the supermarket. Greg's heart didn't race for a while, as if it had made a pact with its owner – beat fast and you admit the worst is possible. Sam had emerged after sixty seconds with a half-eaten doughnut from the bakery section. Greg had smiled.

For a few hours after Celia's failure to arrive home, Greg's heart beat as normal. She's just late, she's just stopped off at the garage. She's with a colleague, having coffee, breakfast, gone all-night-grocery shopping. No need to panic. No need to worry.

But the clock had ticked on, and the phone calls had shed no light, and his heart had no choice but to tell him the truth. She'd had an accident. He could hear it beating, giving him the energy to take action, to find her, help her – because at this stage, it could still be done. Greg's fingers tapped numbers into handsets, his legs carried him along the canal, Ladbroke Grove, the well-lit route she took each week. His mouth spoke assertively to hospital staff and police officers who checked records – no hit and runs, no sightings. No accident.

So she'd obviously run away. His anxiety decreased a bit. Maybe she'd decided to have some space, get away for a night or two. She'd never done anything like this before, but it was possible, wasn't it?

'Has your wife ever had an affair?' asked the female detective in charge of the hunt. She was around forty, of Chinese origin, with a thick cockney accent and a wandering eye. Her name was Vera Oh and she told Greg more personal information than he needed – that she lived alone, that her twenty-year-old son had left home just after his father had. To mark her new life without men, she said, she had given up smoking and taken up pottery and French.

Her left eye's individual approach to *seeing* was disconcerting. Greg didn't know what she was looking at. Was she looking at him? At something over his shoulder? It made him awkward, nervous. Greg didn't realise this was why she'd never had the operation. A wandering eye was more useful for police work than a gun. It disarmed people, made her seem approachable, and caught them unawares.

'Not that I know of,' Greg answered, suddenly less confident of his wife's fidelity.

Still, Vera and her team questioned friends and neighbours. At first, it itched: anger, suspicion, self-questioning. Were we happy? Had she flirted with Dr Tavendale when he'd collected her at A&E that time? Whose number was 07960055911? Why would she have taken her Mini ISA book? The questions were endless, spurred by frenzied attacks on underwear drawers (when had she bought that red silk teddy?), medicine cabinets (why did she use feminine wipes?) and email accounts:

> Hey,
>> Do you eat lamb?
> Ceils x

Hey – a flirty intro, yes? And a kiss at the end? *Ceils*? The email was to Dr Tavendale, who was invited to dinner the following Friday with his wife.

A friend told the police she'd lost weight and dressed better recently. Had she? He hadn't noticed. Was he the kind of husband who didn't notice these sure signs of infidelity? Another friend from school told police Celia had complained that Greg never did the dishes and that sex had become less exciting. And a neighbour had heard an argument at 6.30 one night. Celia had used the word arsehole in front of the children.

The police noticed the older boy, Sam, seemed angry at his mother. 'That's true,' the older boy told Vera Oh. 'She did say arsehole. She doesn't want to come home. She doesn't love us. I'm not stupid!'

None of the happy moments seemed to be relevant anymore. Moments, like 'family story-time' each night, or cooking sausages at the campsite in France, or buying back their old toys at the school fête, or getting too many sweeties at the movies, or the time Johnny told the Bank of Scotland teller that he was FAT HUGE ENORMOUS! Or when the four of them had walked in Kensington Gardens playing I-spy. These moments, and millions of others, seemed to have melted just as Johnny's oversized chocolate ice cream had. A happy, perfect family life, now a sticky puddle on the grass.

'Has your wife ever harmed herself?' Vera Oh asked.

'No,' Greg said.

'Are you sure?'

Was Greg sure of anything anymore? 'She's happy. We're happy.' As if he had to convince himself.

They trawled the canal and other suicide hotspots.

'I told you,' Greg said when the nets, bridges and Samaritans' records drew a blank.

Not long after her failure to arrive home, they found CCTV footage at the garage on her route. She had bought crisps and a *Dr Who* magazine at 4.58 a.m. She had smiled at the checkout person and walked out.

Had she ever arrived at the flat? Greg scoured the five rooms for clues. Had she opened any doors? Put the loo seat down? Dropped her keys and bag in the hall? Turned on a light? It didn't look like she'd arrived. So something had happened between the fifteen minutes or so that it would have taken her to walk from the all-night garage to Queensway Terrace.

Then there was the last option, the one none of them had wanted to embrace till all the others were crossed from the board. She'd been kidnapped, maybe raped, maybe killed, maybe taken somewhere, maybe all of the above.

The other alternatives wandered in and out of the investigation over those five weeks – an accident, a health problem that had caught her unawares, a love affair that made her feel guilty, a sudden depression that she had to bring to an end. But these options were ghost-like, weakening as time wore on.

Greg's heart seemed only to beat fast now when the telephone or the doorbell rang. And then, the dried hard apricot that it had become would fill with blood so fast that it pained him. Even more so when the call was just his Mum, or it was only his friend at the door, and his heart emptied just as fast as it had filled.

Hell was not knowing.

☆

The cat had not come home. And as much as Bobby liked to gallivant, he always came home in the end. The boys lay either side of their Dad in bed. The light in the hall was on, and it shone brightly into the tidy bedroom. Each noise made Sam get up to check the cat flap at the front door. But by 2 a.m. there was no sign, and Johnny was crying so loudly that Greg lost his cool and slapped him on the arm.

'I'm so sorry. Come here.' He cradled five-year-old Johnny under the covers and tried to stop his own tears. This wasn't the father he wanted to be. The one who hit the child for crying over his missing cat and mother. He couldn't hold the tears in. He cried as loudly as his little boy.

Seven-year-old Sam sighed and got out of bed. Did he always have to be the sensible one? Ever since his Mum had ruined their lives by deciding not to come home, he'd had to hold the fort. He'd had to be the one who answered the phone and opened the baked beans and now he was the only one to notice that the Australians across the road were arriving home.

'Let's go and ask them,' Sam said to his crying father and brother.

24

I was sober again. Who were all these people, all these men? What the hell was I doing here?

I stopped at a payphone on Queensway Terrace. Ursula accepted the charges. Her voice felt like a bullbar smashing into me. I'm not sure how the conversation went, exactly, or if it could even be called a conversation, but the gist of it was that I am not an idiot, apparently, but a wonderful girl who may not be ill after all and even if I was, I would cope . . . Probably better if I faced up to it . . . In fact, the hospital had called earlier in the week. She hadn't been told anything, don't worry. When I begged her to stop talking about all that, she said okay, that a bit of fun and laughter till I was ready was just fine, as long as that's what I was doing and not feeling awful all the time.

I asked her to come to London but she was just finishing her final exams. One to go, she said, then she'd be a doctor. 'Anyway,' she said, 'Why would I want to go to England? It's too tame and too green for me. I've got 5,000 bucks saved. When I'm done, I'm going to get a V-dub and drive to Katherine Gorge.'

Dad got on the phone and said pretty much all of the above but in a deeper voice. 'Ring me any time,' he said. 'I love you. We both love you. And we're glad you're having fun. We miss you Bronny, my lovely girl. Please check your email. You are bloody hopeless with email.'

Pete appeared behind the booth. He put his arm around me

and helped me to the house. He took me to my room and lay me on my mattress, then sat beside me as my story exploded.

'Huntington's Disease . . .' Pete repeated.

I hated hearing the name of it.

'Fifty–fifty is not "probably".' He sounded like my Dad.

'What can I do with my life? I can't have kids – I wouldn't do it to them. I can't fall in love. How could I? When all I could offer a man is the pleasure of holding my hand as I die?'

Pete didn't respond with words, but with a lovely long hug.

'I just wonder, what's the point of me? What's the point of me?'

'You know what I think?' He pushed my hair away from my eyes. 'I think it's the *not* knowing that's eating you up.'

We were silent for a moment before we kissed and when we did I forgot all about the rules I'd made on the basin beside the toilet in Kilburn. Angles and lips and teeth and tongues and movements . . . who gave a shit? It just *was*. And I might never have let it end had the doorbell not rung.

I looked at Pete's watch. 'Half-two?' I dragged myself from his arms and went to open the front door. It was Greg from across the road. His thick brown hair was wild, as if something had thrown him around by it in his sleep. The two little boys were with him in their dressing gowns and slippers. Johnny, sleepy and sweet. Sam, serious and angry.

'I'm so sorry,' Greg said. 'The boys have been upset all night and we noticed the lights were on . . . It's Bobby . . . He didn't come home and we thought he might be in your garden again?'

25

'Bobby!' the littlest yelled with the cutest voice I've ever heard in my life. We were in the back yard. Pete had retrieved his torch (he seemed to have everything you'd ever need in his room), but there was no sign of the cat.

'Bobby!' the older, more serious one, called, bumping into the yellow potted eucalyptus tree Pete had bought me. It was dry. I filled a glass and gave it some water.

'Bobby!' Greg yelled.

We scoured the place, but we didn't find anything.

Johnny sat on my lap while Pete made some toast and vegemite.

'Yuk!' Sam said when he saw the brown smears on his toast. 'It's like poo!'

'Your hall smells like poo!' Johnny said sleepily.

'Shhh!' his older brother said. 'Don't be rude.'

Johnny fell asleep in my arms. I'd never been into kids – never had any nieces or nephews or cute cousins to hang out with, and I was surprised how it made me feel, having this warm bunch of snuggledom in my arms. It was beautiful. I found myself looking at Pete as he made toast (without vegemite) and smiling. What would it be like for us to be together, to have a family?

I left Pete to do the dishes and walked across the road carrying Johnny carefully so he wouldn't wake up. I put him in the huge bed in the master bedroom. After I put him down and kissed him on the forehead, I smiled at Sam who was lying in the dark beside his brother and staring intensely at the ceiling.

'Don't worry, he'll come back,' I said.

'You don't know, do you?'

'What?'

'Turn on the light,' seven-year-old Sam ordered.

Johnny was sleeping soundly and Greg was in the bathroom, so I turned on the light.

'Turn around.'

I did as I was told, wondering what the hell could be behind me but a wall or a wardrobe.

There was a wall, and a wardrobe . . . and both were completely covered with newspaper clippings, maps, scribbles and photographs . . . a face was looking at me, a beautiful, happy, smiling face.

'That's my Mummy,' Sam said, pointing to the one that said 'MISSING', then the one that said: 'HAVE YOU SEEN OUR MUMMY?' Then the one that said: 'POLICE CALL OFF SEARCH'.

I sat down on the edge of the bed with my hand on my mouth and looked at her picture. I felt Sam sitting up behind me and moving closer.

I heard Greg come into the bedroom, felt his presence watching me. I turned and held Sam.

'I'm sorry,' I said. 'I didn't know.'

'She doesn't love us anymore,' Sam said.

I held his head in my hands and looked at him. His eyes were not the eyes of a seven-year-old. They were red and tired and sad. One of his front teeth was missing, but he still looked like a downtrodden adult.

'Of course she loves you,' I said.

'If she loves me then why has she done this?'

He was cross-legged on the bed. His serious eyes were begging for an answer.

'Sometimes things happen we have no control over.'

'That's what everyone says.'

'I tell you what, why don't you write to her and ask her? Why don't you tell her you miss her?'

I don't know where this came from. But it seemed to me that he was aching inside and needed some way to get it out.

'No one writes letters anymore and anyway, where would I send it?'

'Do you believe in Santa?'

'I'm not stupid.'

'I know, but do you believe in Santa?'

He paused.

'Yes.'

'Do you write to him?'

'I email.'

'Well I bet your Mum has an email address.'

I looked at Greg, who was still standing in the doorway. He smiled at me and turned on the computer in the corner.

'It's ceils.maher@hotmail.com,' he said.

○

I had a cup of tea with Greg while Sam tapped away on the computer. He told me about the search, which was incompetent from start to finish, he said. Didn't use dogs for days, didn't make use of the media or check airports or ferry crossings or even search the area properly.

'They spent most of the time trying to convince me she'd killed herself or run off with someone.'

'And there's no way?' I asked.

'I adored her. She adored me. We were so happy it's not allowed.'

○

After the tea was finished, we went in to check on Sam. He was in bed asleep. Greg saw that he'd sent an email to his Mum. He opened it and we read it together.

To: ceils.maher@hotmail.com
Subject: No subject
Dear Mummy,

Why did you leave? You are a witch fuck. I hate you and it's all your fault.

I miss you,
Sam

○

As I walked back over to the squat, it dawned on me that their house was fogged by not knowing, a much worse not knowing than mine, because they didn't have a choice. At that moment, I decided that I would ring the hospital first thing in the morning.

26

Death was okay. It was feeling the warmth of the voice that said it's a boy, it's a boy; smelling Greg's coffee as the steam rose from his espresso maker, hearing the sound of Johnny calling to his cat.

The voice of Sam, calling to the cat.

And Greg: '*Bobby, Bobby!*'

If this was death, this was okay. There was no need for head-banging. It was gentle. She would sleep now, she could feel it, and she knew she would never wake up. She began the closing of her eyes.

Is death glimpsing the *Dr Who* slippers of her youngest son?

Or was this real? Were the voices real? Just outside, in the garden?

She was too weak to move fast or far, and the only tool within reach was the cat's head, which she lifted in her tied hands. Swinging her hands, shot-put style, she hurled the sticky head towards the grate, hoping it would clear the opening. It would scare the hell out of them, she thought, but they would get over that. They would never get over losing their Mummy.

It missed, by a lot. The cat's head banged against the wall with a splat, fell to the floor and then rolled out of reach. She began rocking her chair and yelling through the gag, but there were no more slippers and no more shouts of Bobby.

It had probably never happened. She had probably made it all up. She should probably close her eyes now.

✧

Celia would not have picked *The Best of Sex* as the music to die to. The yes and the oh and the yes, yes, yes. It seemed wrong, all wrong, and too long. Her head was swirling. Nothing made sense, but she had to get out of the room, away from the noise. She zigged and zagged slowly to get away. When she finally reached the hall, she put her head against the door of the locked room that she had chipped at with the padlock earlier. Something stank. It made her vomit. She tried to relax so she could swallow and not choke. She hadn't been thinking clearly. Where had her focus gone, falling asleep like that after the cat's head failed to score a goal? She was doing everything in the wrong order, getting confused and . . . THINK, CELIA! Her boys had been outside. Her little boys, calling for their cat. She could not give up. She could not just close her eyes and die.

She reached down over the piece of wood nailed to the floor to pick up the largest piece of shattered ceramic from the lamp.

Why hadn't she smashed the lamp herself while she'd had the energy? She held the ceramic weakly in her bony right hand and cut at her wrist ties, once, twice – forget the blood – three times.

Ten minutes later, she held her hands separately in front of her face. They shook, as did her head, in disbelief. She had done it. Her hands were free.

She tried to untie the knot on her gag, but the pain in the fractured finger on her left hand was agonising and it was impossible to loosen the tight quadruple knot. She grabbed at her gag with her good hand, pulling to free her mouth and yell, but a thick hard crust of blood and pus had meshed with the burnt polyester, and when she yanked she felt as though she was ripping off her face. She moved on to her leg ties but she'd lost momentum, and the cuts on her wrists were excruciating. She wondered if she might faint. She rested.

She'd tried to escape by running up the stairs once before, back in the days when she'd weighed nine stone not six, when she'd had the strength and know-how. The door at the top was locked, she knew that. Anyway, she thought, perhaps the other door in the hall, the locked door, might lead to the real world, or maybe into the hostel next door? This was the door she'd tried to chip at earlier. The chipping had seemed fruitless at the time, but the area around the lock was weakened and loose.

She carefully picked up one of the metal slats that had fallen from the grate, using both hands so she would minimise the pain. She placed it in the crack of the door near to the lock and levered . . . Of course it wasn't going to work. Why would anything work?

It swung open. She pushed the door and watched as a sliver of street-light filtered through a grate and lit up the room.

Celia thought she'd reached rock-bottom – seen hell – but she hadn't; not until she'd looked inside that room.

27

I was obviously not going to be one of those people who could separate sex from emotion. I cried – for the first time in ten years – pretty much the whole way through. I could feel those balls of stone in my tummy eroding a bit, rubbing against each other, dislodging. Even more embarrassing, just after Pete announced that I was officially no longer one of those virgins, I stopped him from moving and said, 'I love you.'

'I'm in love with you too,' he said, looking down at my splotchy face and kissing the tears from it.

'I want to take you home with me.'

I didn't understand the sadness in his stare.

'Let's go home,' I said.

I was also not going to be one of those quiet types. I *yessed* and then squawked like a seagull till we were both floppy. Ten minutes later, I went on top and yelled all over again.

It was good.

It was very good.

I was in love.

And I wanted to dance with the man I loved in the living room.

We took the record player through and played Beatles songs over and over. I played 'Help', using an egg whisk as a microphone and danced on sofas and tables and mattresses. I praised the lord, kissed the Pete, asked him if we could go again.

'Jesus Christ, Bronwyn, we've done it five times already! It'll fall off.'

I felt dejected. I sat down. My bottom lip pouted. I noticed that the song hadn't jumped the way it had when I'd played it in my room.

'The song didn't jump.'

'What?'

'Bear with me,' I said.

I carried the record player back to its position under my bedroom window, plugged it in, put the record on, and played 'Help' again.

It went smoothly the whole way through. I sighed, wondering what the hell I'd been thinking about anyway.

Something about me bending over the record player made Pete confident that he could go a sixth time. I put the track back on and we kissed on the mattress.

'Shhh!'

'What?' Pete asked.

'Shhh! Listen . . .'

I got up and put it on again. It played all the way to that same line, but this time, it didn't jump, it stopped, at exactly the same point: *pleeeeeeeeeeeeeeeeeease heeeeeeeelp meeeeeeeeeeeeeeeee.*

Blump.

Not only had the words descended into creepy slow motion and then stopped with a blump, but the light had gone off at the same time, and when I stood up and tried to switch it back on, I realised that all the lights had gone off. In fact, all the power had gone off.

'You see that?'

All was quiet for a moment. Then I heard Hamish and Francesco coming in from the Polish club and heading for the bong in the living room. I knelt down on the floor, lay face down on the bare floorboards, and listened.

'What are you doing?' Pete asked from his post- and pre-coital position on the mattress.

'Come here!'

Pete lay down beside me and listened to the noises that were undoubtedly coming from the basement. We looked at each other and then pressed our ears to the boards. It was a woman's voice and she was screaming . . .

'HELP ME!

HELP ME!

PLEASE, HELP ME!'

28

When the door to the locked room had opened, Celia had vomited and started to choke. She struggled to dislodge what her stomach had magically managed to expel, grabbed the ceramic she had used to sever her hand ties, and sliced at her face with abandon.

After three huge cuts, the polyester cut in half. She peeled it from her face and spat the bile from her mouth. She coughed. If she'd seen herself, the shock would probably have finished her off. She had a G-force mouth – distorted, rigid, pulled back tight and remaining there. Her right cheek was blistered from the flame that had licked at it. She had cut herself from ear to chin.

Not wanting to throw up again, she slammed the door to the second room. Her body had just found new strength, spurred on by the voices of her family, and by what she had seen in the locked room.

She cut into her legs and freed them. She couldn't walk – she was too weak, and had forgotten how, so she crawled laboriously to the drainpipe and drank as blood spurted from her wounds. She yelled. She heard music coming from another room in the house. She clambered up the stairs and banged at the door. She screamed but the music was too loud. She sat down on the top step for a moment. She may have fainted. The next thing she knew she was at the bottom of the staircase and the music had changed position. It was now coming from the girl's bedroom.

She crawled on all fours into *her* room and yelled up towards the grate on the wall, screaming into the dawn. Blood was spewing from each of the cuts she'd inflicted on herself to be free. She stood for the first time in five weeks and shook as she waited for the right moment to lift the chair and bang it against the ceiling. She felt as though she was lifting a car.

The record jumped. She screamed, but the song had started again, and it was drowning her out. She crawled back to the hall, leaving a trail of thick blood in her wake, opened the door to the stinking room, reached up inside with closed eyes, and pulled the switch on the fuse box.

Everything went quiet.

Celia slumped into her puddle of blood and mustered one last shred of energy from her crumbling body . . .

'HELP ME! HELP ME! PLEASE, HELP ME!'

29

I threw on my netball skirt and polo shirt and raced madly around the ground floor of the house looking for a trapdoor, or some way into the basement. I ran out into the garden and noticed an open grate, and when I knelt down to look inside I nearly threw up. It was a room, covered in excrement, with a chair and broken bits of stuff scattered around. I couldn't see the woman, but there was an open doorway from the room and I could see the foot of a staircase. I ran back inside and opened the hall cupboard. Hurling cans of paint and rolls of wallpaper out into the hallway, I yelled: 'We're coming! We're coming! Hold on!'

Maybe there was an opening underneath the junk, I thought. Hamish and Francesco came out of the living room to see what was going on, then the others walked down the stairs to join them.

I stopped when the back of the cupboard became visible. Shit, why hadn't we found it? It was a normal whitewashed door, inexpertly hidden by some easily movable rubbish.

Hamish kicked the locked door, but he was weak and it didn't budge.

'Pete, you do it,' I yelled. 'Quick!'

He entered the empty cupboard, dressed only in his boxer shorts, took a deep breath, and kicked the door. It fell after one attempt, the hinges bursting from the frame, the door falling and banging down what had to be a staircase.

I went first. The stairs were wooden, banister-less, and sticky. I didn't realise it at the time, but I was walking in blood, my steps leaving red footprints behind me. I got to the bottom of the stairs, stepped over the fallen door, and saw her. A lump on the floor of the concreted, rank hallway. Her eyes were open, staring up at me, but only just, because her bony frame was spewing blood.

'Who was it? I asked. 'Who did this to you?'

She couldn't answer me.

I held her. I could hear Hamish, Pete and Francesco behind me, talking, vomiting at the smell. I closed her wounds with my hands as best I could and yelled at the others to get themselves together, to call the ambulance, fast.

'Who did this?' I repeated.

'Big eyes,' she muttered, over and over as I stroked her sticky hair. 'Big eyes.'

30

Celia's eyes had widened with hope when she heard the door at the top of the staircase being kicked in. At last. Could it be true? Had she beaten him?

But her eyes had closed a little by the time feet descended the stairs. Some people were standing over her. She could hear a gasp and a scream and she could see the faces for a while – three men, and a young woman. They whirled into one vision, as unreal as the world she'd occupied for the last month or so. Faces and clothing and pieces of skin, all blurry and unfamiliar. As she looked up at them, she tried to speak, or at least point, but she was fading, dying probably, and wouldn't that be a shit, after all she'd been through, to not make it after all, to not hear the squeals of her family as they raced to find her, to not even have the strength to point at one of the men looking down at her and say *'Is that him? Is that his voice? There's something in the way he stands.'*

Celia only managed two words – 'Big eyes.' She wanted so badly to manage more than that, to get the monster who'd probably killed her. A wave of frustration swept over her as she heard herself try to speak – she was making rasping noises, nothing else, and the effort hurt so much that in the end she was glad to retreat into darkness.

31

A naked woman was dying in my arms. She looked nothing like the woman I'd seen in Greg's newspaper clippings. Her face was blistered, her finger bone was protruding, her mouth was swollen and cut, her legs ripped to shreds, her tiny frame weak and bony. I looked into her eyes and talked: 'Keep looking at me . . .Your boys are missing you . . .I'm going to get them, Sam and Johnny and Greg, in a minute . . . You're going to get through this . . . You're going to be with them again, be a Mummy and a wife . . . Everything will be fine, just fine . . . Look at me, okay?'

She opened her mouth and tried to say something. She gasped, her tongue huge and bleeding. I could see the frustration in her eyes as she pleaded with me to understand what it was she was trying to say, but after managing the words 'Big eyes', nothing more came.

She closed her eyes as the two paramedics arrived. I didn't want to let her go. I wanted to hold her, to be with her, to will her to live. I felt an overwhelming sense of guilt as I stepped away from her to let the paramedics take over. She'd been underneath my room all that time and I'd been too stoned and too stupid to save her.

✿

I ran up the blood-carpeted staircase, over the floorboards of the hallway, outside, over the street, and banged on Greg's door screaming: 'GREG! GREG! SHE'S ALIVE!'

He opened the door a moment later. He was in his pyjamas. The boys were in their pyjamas behind him.

'She's alive! We've found her! In the basement of my house.'

'What?' Greg said, disbelieving.

'Celia. She's in my house. Alive.'

I would have taken his hand and led him to her, but he was too fast, as was Sam. They were running across the road and into the squat.

'Stop!' I yelled, running after him, holding Johnny in my arms. 'Leave Sam with me! GREG!'

Greg stopped and looked at me, understanding that this meant it wasn't good. He turned to Sam. 'Stay with Bronny,' he said, 'Stay there while I get Mummy. I'll be back out in a minute.'

I held Johnny and Sam on the step of their flat and we looked over the road, just as they had when they'd waited for their cat to come home.

'She must have got my emails,' Sam said. 'I told her if she didn't come back I'd steal Johnny's Tardis.'

I kissed Sam on the forehead. His eyes were different all of a sudden. They were the eyes of a seven-year-old.

Eventually, Greg walked out beside the stretcher and then ran to us while they loaded the stretcher into the back of the ambulance.

'Mummy's going to hospital. Stay with the paramedic till your Gran gets here.'

Greg looked at me for a moment, his eyes squinting a little. He was wondering who I was, who I *really* was. He grabbed Johnny from my lap and handed him to the paramedic. He then steered Sam over to join his little brother. Sam turned his head and smiled kindly at me.

As Greg raced back across the road, I realised I was no longer his friend. I was no longer anyone's friend. I was a squatter from nowhere who had possibly harboured and tortured an innocent woman in the basement.

I ran into the squat. 'Pete!' I yelled. 'Pete! Where are you?' I needed to hold him so badly.

'Down here,' he said.

Reluctantly, I walked down into the basement. Fliss, Cheryl-Anne, Pete, Zach and Hamish were there, staring at something in one of the two rooms. I walked towards them and looked inside the one with the door. It was light now, and I could hear the police cars arriving and I could see what they could see: pieces of paper pinned to the right hand side of the wall, rucksacks and sleeping bags lined up against the left, and two women propped upright in front of me, wrapped like mummies in cling film, their dead eyes staring at us through the plastic.

I fainted.

When I woke, a police officer was standing over me.

32

All seven of them were handcuffed – Bronny, Cheryl-Anne, Fliss, Zach, Hamish, Pete and Francesco – because they were all suspects. They'd been sugar-coated in rucksacks and passport stamps, but now they were to be unpeeled. Two girls had been killed in their drug-littered house. Perhaps a third. And for now, these debauched, homeless, family-less travellers were the only obvious candidates.

Seven . . .

Zach had been handcuffed while still staring at the cling film girls. He was statue-like, frozen. They'd had to drag him from the basement kicking and screaming because one of the girls was his sister. Last time he'd seen her was six months ago at Tullamarine Airport. He'd caught some early waves in Torquay, then jumped in the Land Cruiser. His parents had cried after the picnic had been eaten near Check-in Point 33, and they'd cried even more as their beautiful Jeanie disappeared behind the sliding gates at International Departures. On the way home,

Jeanie's parents phoned her three times. She was still in the passport queue, having a coffee at Gate 11, just boarding, better go, I love you!

They didn't expect her to ring often, but when she stopped altogether after a few months, they began to worry a little. Friends told them they shouldn't. Kids doing the whole indefinite trip thing never ring home. She was probably out of range. They took their friends' advice and relaxed, especially when Zach decided to head off as well. He'd track her down, give her a slap on the wrist, get her to call home for God's sake.

She'd gone to the Royal, he knew that, and Zach was chuffed when Francesco had said he remembered her.

'She went off to a kibbutz I think . . . Don't panic, she'll get in touch.'

So he didn't panic. He got into the lifestyle, playing his guitar and smoking pot and taking cocaine and ecstasy and shagging girls and forgetting to phone home. He laughed when he thought back to how worried he'd been. Now he knew the deal – she, like him, had entered the travel zone, an otherworldly black hole where you forget you even have a family because the people you are with are better than family, more interesting and more interested. And you forget you have a home because wherever you are, whatever room you're sharing with your new family, *is* your home.

But Jeanie wasn't in Israel. She was in cling film.

Zach's handcuffs were taken off not long after he arrived

at the police station. He was no longer a suspect. He was a victim.

Six . . .

Generally speaking, Vera Oh reasoned, girls don't kidnap, rape, torture and kill other girls. Cheryl-Anne might have worked with a man Myra Hindley-style, and the police wondered about this for a while, especially considering her angry racist ideas and the fact that she'd left her three-year-old child in another country just so she could have some fun.

'What sort of woman is she?' Vera Oh had said to her colleague after interviewing Cheryl-Anne McDonald from Wagga Wagga. 'Kind of man-like, y'know?'

But Cheryl-Anne was also the kind of woman who kept a diary, who wrote her comings and goings in elaborate detail, gluing receipts and tickets to the pages, and she had come and gone at all the wrong times to have been involved Myra Hindley-style in any of the crimes.

Cheryl-Anne's handcuffs were unlocked soon after Zach's.

Five . . .

As for Fliss, she'd arrived in London after Celia's kidnapping, and was a blubbering mess, afraid of the dark, never mind blood.

Four . . .

Hamish had been in Ballarat, Australia, around the time of Celia's disappearance.

Three . . . Two . . . One . . .

And then it was Pete's turn, and when they'd finished running his name through the computer they didn't even bother checking Francesco and Bronwyn because Francesco hadn't spent most of his adult life in prison and Bronwyn hadn't hidden a gimp mask under the mattress.

Pete had.

33

As I waited to be released from the station, I thought back to that night at the Polish club. I'd been out of my box on ecstasy, and was rambling on about my new friends – how Cheryl-Anne ate peanut shells; how Fliss wore no underpants even with skirts. I remembered loving them undyingly.

As a kind Asian police officer questioned me about the other suspects, she told me things I'd never known.

Cheryl-Anne had refused to talk to her parents for three years. They wanted her to come home and see her beautiful daughter, but she just didn't feel like it.

I didn't know Fliss's fiancé had chucked her the day before their wedding, that she had come to London, devastated and angry, hoping to make it big as a model so she could return home triumphant, saying: 'Look at me, you bastard, I am a supermodel and even if you beg I will never forgive you!' I didn't know how hard she'd tried to make it, that after hundreds of go-sees and auditions she'd turned to prostitution to get a good set of photographs together, and to keep the diet-amphetamines coming. She'd made quite a name for herself in the area, the police woman said, and was on the brink of being sacked from the Slug and Lettuce for using the storeroom as her boudoir.

I didn't know Zach had enough cocaine in his room to supply a small country.

That Hamish had dropped out of university.

That Pete was a serial killer.

And they'd known nothing about me. Not one of them knew that I had worn death for years; that I had been running away from it and was starting to tire. None of them knew that I'd spent much of my youth watching an old man tend his horses in a disused railway, that when I visited my mother's grave I felt nothing but anger. No one knew that I prayed for the pigs as they shuffled into the bacon factory. No one knew that I had fallen in love. Hopelessly.

I signed some bail conditions. Basically, I wasn't to leave the country till the court case was over. As I scribbled my name, I noticed Pete sitting at a table in an interview room. He was crying. His hands were holding his cheeks and tears were streaming down his face. He caught my eye and shook his head as if to say, 'Not me.' I shook my head: 'Bastard.'

He gestured for me to come over. I saw him ask the officer in his room something. The officer opened the door.

'Miss Kelly?'

'Yes?'

'Two minutes.'

Did I want to go in? Could I sit opposite him, knowing what he'd been accused of, when I could still feel his body on mine, still feel my heart flutter as it had when he'd lain beside me in the park?

My head had decided not to go in, but my body had not obeyed.

We were silent for a long time before Pete spoke.

'I used to steal cars and they deported me. All I've done in this country is try and get home. I've never hurt anyone. I'm not a monster.'

'They say you hid in a coffin at Heathrow.'

'That's not true. Don't listen to them. I'm not what they say I am.'

'Then who are you?'

'I'm Peter McGuire, I'm twenty-four and I'm from a town outside of Adelaide. My mother's a drunk. My father's English. I'm in love with you.'

I think my chair may have fallen on the ground when I stood up to leave, but I didn't look back to check.

34

Bugger. It was very annoying. In fact, it made him short-tempered. If only they'd all gone to bed sooner, not taken that second pill, he'd have sorted it and moved on.

He'd wanted to move on for some time. With the girl in the netball skirt perhaps. But instead of moving on with her, he had found himself standing beside her, looking down at the woman he was *so* over. My God, it was a disgrace, for a girl to get in that state.

He'd felt short tempered as the others gagged at the girl while trying to hold spurting wounds and calling the ambulance and the police and the people across the road. All right, all right, so she seemed to have chopped herself into pieces to get out; so she was naked and brown and red all over. Just get over it already.

He'd felt even more short-tempered at their reaction to the other room. It wasn't anything to faint over, two naked girls wrapped in cling film from head to toe, their eyes looking out like crisp lettuce. It was their own fault. He'd never intended to kill them, but the state they'd gotten themselves into . . . unbelievable. He'd done them a favour, wrapping them. Better that than soggy and stinking, and all right, so it did smell a bit, but not as much as it should have, considering how long they'd been there.

He thought back to when he'd been ill as a boy, and his mother had not come home, had not even phoned to say she'd met someone and would be away for a while. He'd felt really down back then, like taking the pills she'd left in the bathroom cabinet, but then the girl had run by his 12-year-old self's bedroom window. Where was she now? What could he do to make himself feel better? Like he didn't have a brick in his stomach?

He felt as though he could sleep forever.

✿

Pete sat on his concrete bed thinking about the last time he'd been arrested. It was on the Eyre Highway. A police car had been chasing his stolen Jag along the straight flat road for four hours. In the end Pete ran out of petrol just before Ceduna. By the time the police car had caught up and parked beside him, he'd smoked two cigarettes and eaten one apple, core and all.

'G'day,' Pete said to the young cop.

The young cop had not replied.

It was several weeks before Pete had taken his usual seat at court.

'Peter McGuire, you've been found guilty of eighteen charges of car theft, three counts of dangerous driving, thirteen counts of resisting arrest, and four counts of police assault. I have the background report before me and would like to proceed to sentencing without further delay.'

The judge had leafed through the report.

'"Hardly knew real father . . . Mother a drunk . . . Moved from foster home to foster home . . ." A sad tale for the sympathetic reader . . . But then, I'm not a sympathetic reader.'

The judge had looked up at Pete. 'I always found it funny that two hundred years ago they sent people like you over here.

Break the law and they put you in paradise. Well, I'm sending *you* back.'

'What are you on about?' Pete asked.

'Your father is English.'

'He left when I was a kid.'

'That's right. To go back to Cambridge . . . Ever apply for a passport? Ever go to one of those ceremonies where you get all weepy over the anthem?'

'I've lived here all my life,' Pete had said.

'And what a shame that's been for all of us.' He'd smiled. 'I'd buy a raincoat if I were you.'

When they'd dragged Pete down to the cell, he was crying like a baby.

❖

Other than the handcuffs, his journey was much the same as Bronny's, even down to the free booze, which – to his surprise – the air-hostess gave him after the police escort fell asleep. His arrival wasn't much different either. He had no one to meet him, not even a probation officer. He ended up sitting in a small room at the airport with a friendly Scottish Celtic supporter from customs and a not so friendly immigration officer.

'Don't go back,' the immigration officer said when he unlocked Pete's handcuffs. 'Don't even *think* about going back.'

Pete walked out of the Heathrow terminal and stood still in

the rain. He was there for a long time, staring at the grey car park and grey sky and getting very, very wet.

✿

That was six months ago. He'd done a lot since then. Ever resourceful, he'd found the Bayswater underworld almost immediately, and had accumulated all the paperwork he needed to get back home, because getting back home was the only thing on his mind.

His first attempt was mainstream. He got a false Aussie passport, and bought a Qantas ticket with the parts of sixty-three stolen cars.

After that he *did* have a probation officer.

Second time round he was more inventive. False Aussie passport, job-hopping on several cruise liners, then three months in HMP Belmarsh, London for the new offences and the breach of probation.

After his release, he contacted the compliant Celtic-supporting customs official he'd met on his arrival.

'Go cargo,' the official advised. 'I'll arrange it.'

'In a suitcase?'

'Coffin. Big one. I'll drill holes, wrap the corpse clean and tight. Get your supplies in . . . You'll be there in twenty-one hours.'

Pete didn't have two grand, or the stomach, so he decided to take time out. He acquired some references, got a job using the only skill he had – muscle – and thought long and hard about other ways to get back home.

⚬

Funny – Pete thought after Bronny had looked at him with sad, betrayed eyes and then run from the room as fast as she could – getting home seemed completely irrelevant now.

After a while, Pete heard the voices of several officers talking outside his cell. He stood up and pressed his ear against the metal door. They were saying they were worried. They didn't have quite enough. If she woke, one officer said, then they would, but it looked like they might have to let him go. Time was running out.

Pete sat up in bed.

They might have to let him go.

PART FOUR

35

'Bronwyn?'

I was about to leave the police station, but Vera Oh was calling me. 'Your friends left a note.'

'Thanks,' I said, walking outside onto the pavement and reading it.

Bronny,
We're going to the Royal to get our heads together, then we want to find somewhere else to stay. We'll wait for you there.
Fliss and Cheryl-Anne.

Fliss and Cheryl-Anne. The Royal. Did I have the stomach to return there? If I didn't, would I miss them, I wondered, as I walked along a London road in a London suburb filled with Londoners. Would I miss Cheryl-Anne's over-straightened hair? Fliss's flippant approach to life and her regular sexual lessons? Zach's Lenny Kravitz renditions? Hamish's solid advice? Francesco's love of food? Could I go and see them now or would I only ever see them again in a courtroom?

And Pete? My first instincts about him had been right. I should have listened to them. Pete was always there when the noises came, always jumping out at me, scaring me to death. He had tattoos all over and an eerie quietness. His past was a mystery not to be delved into and he had all sorts of tools in his room. The police hadn't told me much, except that he had a list of previous convictions the length of my arm. How could I have been so foolish? To have thought he was kind and gentle and the love of my life when he was a . . . Bloody hell, I'd lost my virginity to a serial killer.

I thought about the days I'd spent in the squat. Celia had been there all along, yelling and banging to get my attention, and I hadn't done anything. If she died, it would be my fault. When I thought about what she'd been through, what the others had been through . . . Oh Jesus. Why hadn't I looked harder in the hall cupboard? Why had I blocked my ears with my fingers and hummed instead of listening properly? Why hadn't I wondered about the shoe, the bloodstain, the jumping record, the smoke, the meowing – then disappearing – cat? If only.

Wandering aimlessly, I found myself standing in front of the squat. The building was covered in plastic and the street was littered with police cars. The occasional onlooker stopped. Inside the Royal next door, I spotted two female backpackers at reception, paying Francesco for a couple of rooms and giggling. I could tell that he was checking them out. I saw Hamish sitting at one of his computers in the Internet café next to reception. I looked down through the basement window of the hostel – ten unfamiliar travellers were drinking and watching MTV.

A new wave had come and flattened the sand.

I had almost decided to go inside, to touch base with Fliss and Cheryl-Anne, and maybe go somewhere safe with them.

'Your passport was in there.' I jumped, scared out of my wits, then turned around to see Zach.

'And your shoulder bag, pinned to the wall. Did you see it?'

It took me a moment to understand what this meant. My passport, which had been stolen from my hostel room the day after I'd arrived in London, was pinned in that horrible room alongside the passports and tickets of dead women.

'I'd have been next,' I thought out loud.

36

In the Cromwell Hospital Greg sat beside his wife's bed. Much of her face was bandaged and two drips were attached to her arm, one filled with blood, the other saline. She was still in a coma.

'And at the bottom he wrote, "I'm sorry I was angry, I miss you. Love, Sam." . . . Spelt the right way and all. I put it on the mantelpiece, in the living room. I've been very tidy, just as you like it . . .'

He knew he was rambling, but he'd been talking to her

bandaged face all day, and it was hard to converse with a lifeless woman, especially when he'd been told to expect the worst, and when he felt so angry at himself for letting it happen. Why did he let her convince him it was okay to power-walk home at that hour? Why did he not search the area more thoroughly himself, knock on doors, for God's sake? Why had he not followed the cat? He might have found the shoe in the skip, or in that girl's room. Might have heard the noises she'd been making, poor Ceils. What had he done to her? What had she been through?

A counsellor – female, six feet two, and with the evidence of a child's breakfast on her shirt – came to see Greg a few hours after they'd stitched and bandaged Celia. He would get through it, the woman told him. He would find the strength. And Celia would get through it too. Her scars would heal.

'But what about the ones inside?' Greg asked.

'Your love – and the boys' cuddles – will heal those . . . Go home and rest,' the counsellor told him. 'They'll ring if there's any change.'

✿

The boys were at home with all four grandparents, an aunt and an uncle. They were supposed to be watching the television but they were really watching the phone. If it rang, it would mean she was either alive or dead. The television had far less power about it, but still Dr Who's *The Girl in the Wardrobe* blared in a vain attempt to divert everyone from self-punishment.

Sam pinched himself on the leg for not *knowing* that she was there, for being angry with her for not coming home, and for blaming her for disappearing.

Celia's Mum ground her teeth for not offering to pick her up on Tuesday mornings when she was always awake at that hour anyway.

Her Dad wished he'd offered to help them with the mortgage so she didn't have to work.

Her brother wondered why he'd not given them the car he never used, an old Volvo that he hadn't got around to selling. She could have driven to the hospital.

Her sister-in-law could have helped Greg knock on doors when he'd asked for help after the search was called off. Why did they tell him to move on for the sake of the boys?

Many people pondered similarly, absorbing guilt in the airwaves that did not belong to them:

Detective Inspector Vera Oh, whose own failed marriage had made her doubt Greg's constant assertion that he and Celia were happy.

The lowly cops who'd searched the street and not found the trainer in the skip.

The neighbour who'd said she'd heard Celia say arsehole in front of the boys.

The colleague who'd repeated Celia's lamentations about sex losing its oomph.

The bloke who'd walked down Queensway Terrace just after

she'd been taken. He had seen a man looking under a Honda Jazz. Why had he not told the police?

The hotelier behind the squat who'd noticed someone moving about the garden in the middle of the night before the squatters had moved in.

And so it went on. Guilt everywhere, except where it belonged.

⚬

Greg wanted to believe the counsellor. He even told himself that if she woke up and smiled at him in the midst of her bandages, then maybe it was true, maybe they could be happy again.

'I can't leave,' Greg told the counsellor. 'I have to be with her if she wakes up.'

'*When* she wakes up, you'll scare her to death with that hair,' the counsellor said. Greg looked in the small mirror. She was right. His hair took up more space than his head, reaching for the sky in thick wads.

'Go home, have some rest and a shower. We'll phone you.'

The phone outside Celia's hospital room rang. A fat nurse with a Welsh accent answered it. 'No, there's no change,' she said.

Greg looked at the counsellor and sighed. He supposed the police were almost as eager as he was for her to wake up. She could identify him. They were pretty sure they had the guy, but Celia's evidence would be the clincher. Greg thought about the man who'd done this to his wife. The bastard had helped

Greg stand up after he'd slipped on the blood. Greg had actually thanked him for calling an ambulance. He had no. 1 hair, boxer shorts, muscles and tattoos. Did he have big eyes? The girl, Bronwyn, had told police that Celia's last words were 'Big eyes . . .' Were his eyes big? He couldn't remember.

'Okay,' Greg told the counsellor. 'I'll go get some rest.'

37

Zach decided to stay at the Royal, but after he'd told me about my shoulder bag and passport, I had an even more overwhelming urge to get away from there. As far as I knew, Fliss and Cheryl-Anne were still there waiting for me. But I couldn't go in. Couldn't be near the place where I had touched and loved Peter McGuire, the place where I had failed to save Celia and where I would have been next.

As I watched Zach walk down Queensway Terrace I thought about his sister's return journey. She wouldn't get drunk on Bacardi and Coke and touch up her makeup from the Murray River onwards, excited and nervous about seeing everyone again. She'd be all alone in a dark box in a freezing hold alongside suitcases and skis. And she wouldn't arrive to the delighted squeals of her family as they marvelled at how healthy (fat) she looked. Instead she and her box would be taken to a quiet room until the paperwork was done.

Oh God, it was the darkness, wasn't it? Coming after me.

As I wandered down Queensway I regretted being too embarrassed to ask Zach for some money. I had none. Not a penny. I'd been getting by on Hamish's loan and other people's bread and peanut butter and now that I had no people in my life, I was screwed.

Where could I go? I was penniless, exhausted and starving.

I found myself heading for the Porchester. They hadn't paid me yet. My wages and my bonus were due next week, so I decided to see if the boss was on a late shift and ask for an advance. After all, it wasn't so very long ago that I had been Employee of the Week.

The door to the steam rooms was closed. It was only 9 p.m. and should be open for another hour. I knocked, but there was no answer. I went around to the other side of the building and entered the main reception area. The gym and pool were bustling with customers, but the door leading through to the steam rooms had been boarded over and was being painted.

'Why are the steam rooms closed?' I asked the pretty receptionist who'd chatted up Pete not long ago.

'It's been shut down,' she said. I noticed she was staring at me as if *I* was the serial killer.

I walked past the notice board – at some point my photo had been replaced by one of Esther, the new Employee of the Week. I walked up to Nathan's office and knocked on his door. He was still in after a busy day closing down the steam rooms and finding jobs for most of the employees. But he didn't have a job for me, or any money. He had three other things: the letter I'd half-written to Ursula and left at the towel desk, in which I'd called him a knob-head; the purse I'd been accused of stealing, which was found in Pete's locker; and some advice:

'Get out of my office. I should have listened to Esther. Get out!'

✧

Okey-dokey, I thought to myself, skulking down the stairs. Esther and Kate had obviously heard I was around, and had come out to see me off. They stood in line with the receptionist who had fancied Pete, each of them spitting at me with their eyes, as I walked slowly out of the Porchester.

I needed to find somewhere safe for the night so I could think about what to do next. I wasn't allowed home yet – I was a material witness – and I had no idea what I would do till it was all over.

I sat on a step across from the steam room entrance. It was dark and quiet there and if I pressed my face into my knees I could almost make myself invisible. The street reminded me of Bucks Row, where Pete said a woman had been found in 1888. The killer had slit her throat and kept a bit of her. God, I had been so stupid! It was creepy and still – a dead end at the bottom of Queensway – but every now and again someone walked by. Staff from the Porchester. Clients in Lycra. A man and a woman, chatting. A man, alone. Two men – were they the shady men who'd told me when to get out of the squat on the night of the housewarming? A guy with a hoodie – was he Bobby Rainproof, who I'd bought dope from at the Polish Club? My God, the underworld was everywhere, a world that until recently had seemed fun, was now scaring the living shit out of me.

I wasn't permitted to get my jeans or anything out of the squat, so I still had my netball skirt and polo shirt on. It was getting cold. The gym and pool section of the Porchester had shut by now and the street was deserted. Rubbing my arms with my hands, I remembered that I still had the keys to the steam rooms pinned to the inside of my polo shirt pocket. In his fury, Boss-man Nathan had forgotten to ask me to return them.

A man on a scooter whooshed by. I watched him disappear around the corner, then raced across to the huge corner door. The key opened it easily. I shut the door behind me and locked it from the inside; peeking out the keyhole to make sure no one had seen me, then replacing the key in the hole.

It was dark in there. I didn't want to put on any of the lights in case anyone outside noticed, so I walked past reception, grabbed a jug of water from the kitchen, drank half and gave the other half to the dry bamboo palm, took some bread from behind the counter, and went through the double doors into the huge relaxation area. The loungers were still laid out around the room. I checked the bright digital clock behind the towel dispensary desk. It was after ten. Chewing the stale bread, I took two towels from behind the desk and sat down on one of the loungers. But I couldn't get warm.

I walked back to the reception booth by the front door and turned on the computer. The light from the screen lit up the huge mirror on the wall opposite the booth. It must have been about eight feet by eight feet. Not surprisingly, I looked wired to the moon. I googled Internet Café, Queensway Terrace, then dialled Hamish's number – a mobile – and praised the lord when he answered.

'Hey you,' he said. God, his voice was just what I needed. Gentle and kind and sensible. 'Honey, calm down. Don't worry,' Hamish said. 'Everything's fine now. It's all over.'

When I hung up, I felt a wave of relief. Soon Hamish would come and hug me and reassure me that everything was going to be okay. But in the meantime, this place was bloody freezing.

I walked across the marble floor, down the sweeping staircase that wrapped itself around the small tear-shaped plunge pool and past the showers and full-length mirrors across from them. Some street-light trickled in from a high window in the body-scrub room opposite the showers. It looked even more like a torture chamber without the lights on. I wondered where Mitt-woman would go now. How much demand was there for mitt-women? The floor hadn't been hosed, so piles of skin crumbs coated the surface. I walked round the corner to the steam rooms and saunas. It was dark in the bowels of the building, but I remembered that there were two saunas on one side and two steam rooms on the other, with a cleaning cupboard at the end. I felt my way around the wall, looking for the switch box beside the cupboard that Esther had told me I was not qualified or trained to touch, and finally found it. I opened the small metal door, pressed down a switch and waited to see if anything happened. There was nothing for a moment – just darkness – then one of the saunas began to glow. I moved towards it, and tried to open the glass door, but it was locked. So I went back to the control box and fumbled for some keys that were on hooks on the inside of the metal door. After trying three, I finally found the right one, and opened the glass door of the sauna.

Once inside, I put the sauna key down beside the copper bucket of water and spooned some water on top of the coals. They sizzled, then steamed. I stood over the glowing coals rubbing my hands, until a creaking noise frightened me – it was like a sinking ship. As I crept out of the sauna, a rat scuttled past my feet. I screamed, ran back past the body-scrub room and showers, up the stairs by the plunge pool, through the relaxation area, out of the double doors, past the kitchen, and into reception.

I dialled my home number. The numbers seemed beautiful, familiar, safe.

'Ursula!'

'Bron, how are you? How's London?'

Oh dear, my voice was getting shaky. 'I love you. I just wanted to hear your voice.'

'You sound flat.'

'I wish I was. I'm over nine stone. It's the peanut butter and lager.'

'You have an accent.'

'I do not.'

'I'll wire some money. Email me the bank details.'

'I miss you!'

'You're upset! Bronny, talk to me.'

'I'm fine. It's just, I don't know.'

Suddenly everything inside me churned. I felt confused. Thoughts and images whirled in my head. Had all this really happened? Had I really fallen in love with a man who killed people? Had I really ignored the screams of a tortured woman? Did I really have a fifty–fifty chance of dying?

Of course, Ursula and Dad only knew about that last whirling query, and assumed it was only this that was making me upset.

'Bron, you need to ring Dr Gibbons. This is ridiculous. Get it over with.'

'I'm scared.'

'We're here.'

'I feel worthless.'

'You're worth more to us than anything. We love you. Listen to me, Mum had a good life. She and Dad loved each other, and us. You'd cope, we'd all cope, together.'

'But for twenty years I'd be dying.'

'In the worst-case scenario, for twenty years you'd be living, which is more than you're doing at the moment . . . Dad wants to speak to you.'

He must have been sitting on Ursula's lap . . . 'Bronny, I have something for you. Have you got a fax there?'

I checked and beside the computer there was a fax machine. 'Yes.'

'What's the number?'

'I looked on the sticker on the machine and read it to him, then switched the machine on.'

'I was supposed to give it to you after the result, but you ran away . . . It's from Mum.'

I was silent, waiting. Mum was about to speak to me. She was going to say something I'd not heard her say before, from a single piece of white paper. I gulped, and watched the fax's 'on' button flash red. She's coming, she's coming . . . she's here.

The sheet of paper oozed out of the machine. I could see the shadow of her ghost-writing as traces of it appeared line by line through the other side.

'She wanted you to read it afterwards, after you've got the result,' Dad said.

I wanted to yell: 'Don't give me this dead woman's letter, it's fucked up!' I wanted to yell: 'No! This has nothing to do with the spinning coin. I've just escaped from a psychopath!'

But the whole page had landed face down in the paper holder.

Dad waited for me to say something, but I didn't.

'Bronny?'

'Yeah?'

'Are you okay?

'Yeah.'

'I love you.'

'I love you too . . . I'm going to ring the hospital now.'

'Call us straight after.'

'Yeah.'

I hung up and looked at Mum's letter. She'd wanted me to read it after the result. Dad wasn't supposed to give it to me till then. But here it was, words from my dead Mum, the person I'd thought about each hour, each day, who'd left me alone to endure a terrible wait. I'd been waiting ever since. I'd done enough of it.

I took the letter from the machine and read it.

Hey Winster,

I'm sitting on the veranda watching you ride your trike up and down. We've just worked out together that you're going to be four in 79½ days! You have curly hair and a huge toothy smile.

I'm the petrol-station keeper and when you stopped to fill up, I grabbed your happy chunky cheeks and kissed you.

I'm not with you now, am I? I'm not there to help you with this. I'm so sorry.

I was eighteen. My Mum took me because Dad wasn't feeling well. I remember how it felt to this day. The before and after, and you know I'm not sure if before was better than after. Was it? I was devastated. But then it felt as if I'd been given a new set of legs. You learn to walk again – different, but again.

Was it wrong for me to fall in love with your father? I hadn't planned on it, but when he walked me home from the Chocolate Association Ball there was nothing either of us could do about it.

Was it wrong getting pregnant that first time? Seeing Ursula's bright eyes smile at me (I was sure of it) long before they were supposed to be able to?

And having you?

. . . Sorry about that, you fell off your trike and I had to put a Band-Aid on your knee. You're riding even faster now. I do hope you never lose that wild spirit of yours.

I'd thought about doing a video, but then I imagined you watching it over and over, rewinding and fast forwarding, and I didn't like the idea of you doing that. So I'm writing this instead so that you can feel me with you when it's time. I'm with you, my little girl. I'm with you. And it's going to be okay.

I am a lucky person. Blessed. I love you.

Forever your Mummy

XXXXXXX

I folded the letter and put it in my pocket. Then I googled the hospital, and dialled the number.

'He's not in yet . . .' the nurse said.

I read out the digits on the Porchester telephone, replaced the handset, and turned off the computer. Dr Gibbons would ring me back in an hour.

In an hour, the twenty-cent piece would land.

38

Room 1, Celia's room, was at the end of the second floor, just beside the fire escape. It was the Intensive Care Unit, lined with seven rooms on each side, with a nurse's station in the centre. No police guarded Celia because the perpetrator was behind bars and there was nothing to worry about. There was only one other patient on the entire floor so it was quiet and empty except for the occasional phone-answering and drip-checking of one beefy nurse.

The beefy nurse wore a uniform a size too small. As a result, the button at the front of her hefty bosom was permanently undone. The patient in room 12 had the privilege of seeing down and into her GG bra as she bent over him to change his dirty hospital gown. It wasn't only the greying bra that made the patient unlucky, but the gush of air that wafted from it, a stale bosom smell the recovering heart attack patient had never smelt before, and which made him wonder if his ticker might just go again. She adjusted his fresh white gown, smiled, and left him to try and sleep.

It wasn't long since Greg had left the hospital. He'd dithered about, coming in and out, in and out, afraid to go, and in the end the counsellor from floor seven had practically pushed him into the lift.

'Promise you'll ring!' Greg said, as the counsellor pressed the lift button behind the nurse's station.

'Promise,' the beefy nurse and the tall counsellor said in unison, watching the lift doors close behind Greg's large unkempt hair.

'Tea?' Beefy asked Tall.

'Home,' the lanky counsellor said, taking the stairs, which she always did to avoid awkward patient-client lift silence – or worse – chat.

The nurse drank her tea in peace, flicking through *Heat* magazine, taking special interest in a story about breast reduction. She put her magazine down when she heard a whimper coming from room 1.

✿

Celia had opened her eyes. It had been so long since she'd opened them to anything pleasant – the ceiling of her happy bedroom, the faces of her happy sons, the direct light of a happy sun – that she assumed it was either a dream or death. Each time she'd woken recently, there had been a moment of unawareness, where she did not know where she was, and then the smell and the pain had brought the reality to her, that she was a tied, dying sexual plaything.

There was a large nurse standing over her. Was she imagining her, as she had imagined Greg so often over the last five weeks? She'd conjured her husband's kind eyes and loving smile, imagined the gentle comfort of his hand on hers, the smooth deep sound of his lovely Scottish voice. She managed to smile at the face of the nurse. She moaned a soft, happy moan; still thinking this was not real.

'I'm going to ring the doctor, and Greg. I'll get him and the boys. They'll be here any minute. Oh my goodness!'

The nurse ran out of the room to ring several phone numbers.

The beefy nurse did not return, but after a while a doctor did, dressed in surgical mask and gown. Still unsure as to whether she was awake or indeed alive, Celia looked down to check herself. She saw white sheets. She lifted the top sheet with her bandaged hand and saw her bandaged body. She felt her face with her hand, covered in cloth except for eyes, nose and mouth. Then she looked up at the doctor again. This was real. She had made it.

Things came into focus better. The room was filled with flowers and cards. The window had a view of the city. The floor was clean and bright, except for the unconscious nurse lying in the doorway.

'You almost had a lucky escape, didn't you?' the man said.

39

After the initial scare of being arrested and questioned, he was allowed to leave the police station, free to go. He smiled as he walked out of Paddington Green, sure he had it all sorted. Kill her before she talked, then head off. He'd found a car and bought a ticket and just had this one thing to do before leaving for a fresh start. He felt so confident and relaxed that he took his time walking up to the second floor. But somewhere between ground and first he remembered the blood and sperm. She may have been wiped or washed a little, but he was probably in every frigging nook – nose-blood from when she'd kicked him, sperm from the many times he'd ejaculated on or in her. Shit. He was usually so thorough – took care to clean things up – and even though they'd taken his fingerprints and DNA, he felt confident that the two dead ones in the cling-film would reveal nothing. But he'd had no time to do that with this one, what with Bronwyn finding her the way she had.

He realised the woman would lead the police to him alive or dead. And even though he'd found a car and bought a ticket, they'd track him down eventually, put in all their resources, because they would have more than enough evidence.

He thought on his feet, sneaking into a vacant operating theatre on the first floor for some materials, then heading back up to IT.

❖

It was the nurse's fault, questioning him like that.

'Doctor?' she'd said, hanging up the phone at her nurse's station and waddling up behind him. 'That was quick! Excuse me, isn't it wonderful, Doctor!'

He excused her all right, with a wallop that sent her impossible cleavage to the floor.

He moved the nurse inside and shut the door to room 1 carefully, marvelling at his ex, whose eyes were open but staring blankly, as if she didn't believe she was seeing anything at all. It had been over for a long time, he thought, as he placed a layer of thick surgical tape on her swollen mouth, which he then covered with a cloth mouth guard. Encouraging her to stand up with a scalpel to the eye, he ripped the drips from her arms, put her in a wheelchair, and pressed the down button of the lift, with the scalpel firmly pressed against the back of her neck.

When the doors opened, there was a young nurse in the lift. His heart stopped for a moment, realising he looked odd with his surgical mask on. Also, his patient was wriggling in her chair, but he wheeled it inside and said: 'Yes, I know, the painkillers will kick in soon,' while making an incision in Celia's neck that was big enough to stop the wriggling.

'Poor thing,' he said to the young nurse through his cloth mask. 'She's been like this for hours.'

He said cheerio on the ground floor before heading down to the car park. It was quiet, and he had parked out of sight of the security cameras, so he felt fairly confident that no one had seen him bundle her into the boot and smash her over the head with the jack.

Problem was, once in the car, he had no idea where to take her. She was dead, or near as, he was sure of it. He just had to find somewhere to clean her up, then he could leave as planned.

He found himself driving to Queensway Terrace, which was a stupid thing to do – what was he thinking? But he didn't know where else to go. He parked down the road from the Royal and the squat and watched the activity around the crime scene. He almost felt proud, looking on as swarms of detectives and forensic specialists scoured the site.

There was a bang. Was it coming from the boot? Jesus, surely not. This one was unbelievable. She just would not get the hint. Not like that dirty rat who'd given up the ghost still reasonably fresh, or Jeanie with her surfer's chick shark tooth who *decided* to die early on. He hadn't killed them, hadn't needed to, they'd just stopped breathing after a while, bless.

It was coming from the boot.

'Think!' he said to himself. 'What is wrong with you? Make a decision. Jesus Christ. All I need is a place to tidy up.'

He put the key in the ignition and turned it, but then seemed unable to remember what to do next. He pushed the brake instead of the clutch, put the gear in reverse instead of first. Held the key for so long the engine flooded. He was losing his mind. It was the stress, probably.

Was that his phone ringing?

40

The adults in the room had stood up slowly as Greg held the phone in silence. The children had stood up too, clinging onto the loose clothing of a nearby adult.

'She's awake!' Greg yelled.

There was screaming and hugging and jumping about, eyes and mouths suddenly relaxed, muscles unknotted. Tears became happy tears.

Keys and boys' trinkets were grabbed, cars gotten into, and one or two of Celia's family may have laughed, for the first time in five weeks.

The drive was only five minutes, but it seemed to take hours. Getting the boys buckled in, turning the key, waiting for a red Fiat to turn right at Queensway, stopping at three sets of traffic lights.

Greg's car was first to arrive. It zoomed into the underground car park, driving over a jack that someone had left lying in the middle of the concrete, and bumped back down to earth. He swerved into a space, undid his seatbelt, opened the back door, undid the boys' seatbelts, shut the doors, and ran.

○

Who arrived first? Who was faster? The little boys, striding up the stairs to the second floor with their drawings and *Dr Who* cards? Greg, running behind them, laughing? The parents and the brother and sister-in-law, pressing the button on the lift too many times? It was hard to know, because they all remembered seeing the same thing at exactly the same time: a doctor whose tardy response to the news of Celia's wakening may have saved his life, a confused nurse in the doorway of room 1 . . .

. . .and an empty bed.

41

After giving the telephone number to the hospital, I shivered. It was ice-cold, and the creaking-ship noise that I'd heard downstairs seemed to be getting louder. When I exhaled, the air in front of me fogged. I opened the double doors and grabbed one of the white towels I'd used earlier. I wrapped it around me and walked across to the stairs, and down towards the sauna. I had to get warm. But the closer I got to the sauna, the louder the creaking noise became, and I found myself acting like one of those idiots in the movies who go towards said terrifying noise, instead of running as fast as they can away from it.

It was coming from the cleaning cupboard downstairs. I got some keys out of the metal cupboard and tried a few before finding the right one. I pushed the door slowly, tip-toed into the small dark cupboard, walked past the *schmeissing* sticks, cleaning fluids and rat poisons, and stopped in front of a deafening boiler labelled 'showers'. I switched the 'off' button and the creaking stopped. Thank God, I thought as I exhaled.

When I turned around, Hamish was standing in front of me.

I screamed, of course, not just once, but twice. An instant-reaction-high-pitched scream, then an I'm-not-ready-to-stop-screaming-yet one.

After Hamish had calmed me down, he laughed and said he'd be asking me for the dry cleaning bill. It was such a relief seeing Hamish. He said and did all the right things.

'Let's have something to eat,' he said, putting his arm around me and leading me back upstairs.

He had brought bread and peanut butter, my favourite, which he set out on the desk as I tried to get warm with three towels or so.

The guy was a nutcase, or so Hamish said, with a huge list of previous. He'd been deported, breached probation, failed to appear at court – and so on and so on.

'Hamish, it's not just Pete. There's something I need to tell you.'

'What is it darlin'?'

'The phone's about to ring.' I said, telling him who was going to ring and why.

He stopped spreading the peanut butter and held me tightly. 'It's okay, it's okay, I'm here.'

☼

The phone felt like it had rung inside me. I gasped. After years of thinking about this moment, it had come. Our embrace froze. We moved away from each other, took a deep breath, then walked hand in hand towards the reception area.

It was Dr Gibbons with the test results.

The wave of terror he unleashed pelted into me full blast. I let go of Hamish's hand. He spoke for a while, longer than I thought he would, and I sat facing the back wall listening, just taking it all in. He was a kind man, always had been.

'Are you there?' he asked, because I hadn't said anything for a while.

'Um . . .' I couldn't answer the lovely doctor, because I wasn't really sure if I *was* there, or anywhere. I stood up to check if I was, to look at myself in the mirror opposite reception, to touch my face and watch my reflection as some kind of proof that I was in this place, that I had just heard what I had heard. I turned around and faced the mirror. But it was too dark, I couldn't see anything. I stared at the darkness for a moment, then said: 'Yes, I'm here. I'm fine, thanks. No, I'm not alone. Yes, I will. Bye Doctor. Thanks,' and hung up.

Then noises came from me that I didn't know I could make. They weren't happy ones. I had the Huntington's gene. I was going to die a horrible death, like Mum had. I was going to get clumsy. Shit, I had already gotten clumsy. I had tripped over on the pavement, banged my head on the fridge. And this is what it would be like from now on. I would wonder if a paper cut meant it had started, if a forgotten phone number meant it had. And maybe it had, already.

I was going to lose control of my body, make weird angry movements that scared people away. I was going to forget things and choke and die. I was never going to love someone properly, or have kids. When the time came, Ursula would be married or camping in Katherine Gorge. Dad would be old or dead and I'd die alone, with no one loving me, no one holding my hand. Please bring back the not knowing. Please bring back the not knowing.

I fell to my knees and banged my fists against the marble. I screamed and yelled and moaned and wriggled on the floor like a half-squished ant. 'NO!' I didn't want to die. I wished I'd never phoned. I should never have phoned. Not knowing *was* better than knowing this terrible thing was in me, part of me, ahead of me. It was so fucking unfair! Why me? All the things people say, I said through my yells, meaning them as much as people always mean them. It's so unfair. I was just eighteen. I'd had a shitty, pointless life so far, and it was only going to get even more shitty and more pointless. Why fucking me?

Hamish gathered me in his arms on the floor and held me as I screamed. I think I kept going for a long, long time, but eventually the yelling and crying became sobbing, shuddering, softer somehow.

I had cried in bed with Pete, but not enough to make up for the years I hadn't, just enough to disturb the stones in my stomach a little. Now I could feel them rubbing and eroding and melting completely, balls of Maltesers in a hot steaming pot. I remembered the tone of Mum's letter: she sounded happy, said she was lucky. She'd kissed my chubby cheeks.

I saw the letter on the bench at reception, made my way towards it and re-read it, touching the words with my fingers, taking in what Mum was trying to tell me – that it would be okay, that she was with me, that she loved me.

'Learn to walk again,' I read.

'What?' Hamish asked me. Poor Hamish. He'd been watching me grieve, unsure what to do, how to respond.

'My Mum wrote this letter to me. She said finding out is like getting a new set of legs, and that I'll learn to walk again. I didn't know what she meant a few minutes ago.'

'She means you should fight,' Hamish said.

'That's it.'

She was right. I should fight. I should fight for the years I'd been given, for the friends I could make and the fun I could have and the risks I could take and the places I could go. For the love I could give.

My stomach began to feel like a stomach for the first time in ten years and not a sack of rocks. I listened to my heartbeat. It was loud and fast. Everything about me seemed poised. A surge of adrenaline was running through me. I hadn't felt this in a while. My first expedition into life had been numbed by cannabis so I had still been anaesthetised. Despite declaring dramatically that I was going to *live,* all I'd done was run away. What had been the point to me? Employee of the Week? (Spectacularly disgraced.) Friend of the Year? (To kindred spirits who fucked off just as fast as they fucked on.) Root of the Century? (To a serial killer! Ha!) What about Saviour of the Universe? I hadn't even heard Celia. I'd done nothing, made no imprint.

But now I knew I had fewer years to make one, something started to bubble as if my family's life-ban from Luna Park had been lifted, and I had been given another all-day ticket. Now I wanted that ticket. I wanted to queue at the Scenic Railway, get in the first carriage beside Ursula, put my arms in the air, open my eyes wide and yell. I had just been given a day of limitless stomach-churning rides that would end, of course, but would leave a knowing smile on me because I had ridden them, Scenic Railway and all. Mum and Hamish were right, I had to fight. I *would* fight. I would start living properly, now I knew I was dying.

'That's the spirit,' Hamish said, handing me a bag of clothes to change into.

'Have a shower. I'll go buy some wine and we'll have a drink to the rest of your life.'

✿

I took Hamish's poly bag of clothes and walked downstairs. I needed to calm myself before ringing Ursula and Dad. Did they have to go through all of this again? And then there was the guilt they'd feel – Dad for loving a woman who gave this to me, Ursula for being the one who got away.

More tears came as I stood in the shower cubicle waiting for the water to heat up. I pressed my hands against the shower wall and waited. But the water didn't heat up and I remembered that I'd turned off the showers in the cupboard. I wrapped a towel around myself and walked out to the cupboard, switching on the boiler again. I raced back to the shower, closed the door and hung up my towel. After a few seconds, I stood under the hot water and washed my hair, scrubbed my legs, arms and torso, cleaned everywhere, rubbing the badness of everything away – Pete and the squat, that poor woman, me . . .

I'd only remembered bad things about Mum for years, had only ever thought of her as an ill person and the cause of my unhappiness, but now bunches of images came back to me. Of making fairy cakes in the kitchen and accidentally getting cream all over Mum's green jumper. Of throwing up at my seventh birthday party and proclaiming: 'The jelly must be off!' when I'd eaten twenty-three sausage rolls, twelve violet crumbles and half an elephant-shaped ice-cream cake beforehand. Of the two of us watching *Anne of Green Gables* with the curtains shut, spooned together on the huge leather sofa. Of getting a celebratory lunch at the Red Lion when, aged nine, I'd won Best and Fairest in the St Patrick's netball team. Of spending the day at Mum's work – she was a GP – and announcing carefully that 'Jane Beaumont is here for her 11 o'clock, Dr Kelly.' Of reading *Ping* and *Seven Little Australians* and *The Magic Faraway Tree*. Of singing: 'Little Lucy Locket, She's got an empty socket, She'll keep an eye open for ya!'

Of laughing.

I dried myself, wrapped the towel around me, and went out to the full-length mirrors opposite the showers. The mirrors were steamed up, so I slowly rubbed one with my hands.

My face looked terrible.

I walked into the body-scrub room, which was dimly lit by the street-light from the window Hamish had obviously prised open to get in. The coating of dead skin on the floor had Hamish's footprints on it and looked spooky. Flicking brown skin from my bare feet, I grabbed the polyester bag of clothes Hamish had brought for me, stopped, and thought for a moment.

I took the bag of clothes and went back out to *really* look at myself in the mirror.

I looked exhausted from running. I had nothing to run from anymore. Oddly, my features seemed more relaxed now that I knew for certain. I dropped the towel to the floor and stared at myself – at the body I'd always been scared of. A good body, good shape, pretty. Looking at it you'd never know there was a worm gnawing away inside.

Reaching into the plastic bag, I grabbed Hamish's T-shirt and put it on. The mirror had steamed up. I rubbed a patch to fix my hair, looked at my sad though relaxed face. I rubbed a bit lower to look at myself in the white T-shirt Hamish said he used to wear to bed – size sixteen maybe, nice seams, low round neck, and with a sweeping black drawing on the front of two very big eyes.

PART FIVE

42

It had all gone to fuck, Hamish thought. His own fault. Should have stuck with the drifters who had less to live for. Should have stopped the squatters moving in. He felt sicker by the minute.

When Bronwyn had phoned, he'd been parked in Queensway Terrace wondering how best to deal with the body. He had his 'working clothes' in plastic bags on the passenger seat.

He didn't only need to dump it, he needed to clean it, so there'd be nothing to lead the police to him. As if by magic, Bronwyn rang with the answer. The steam rooms. More chemicals and scrubbing brushes than he'd know what to do with. Hell, there might even be one of those crematorium-like furnaces.

After dealing with the body, he would run away. He'd run away before, after the year he'd done because of the tennis player in Toronto. He'd liked the girl, and had watched her often, the battered curtain of his student room his mask, but one night he followed her home and he got the year. It had felt nice, made him throb a little thinking about it now.

But no time for reminiscing, Hamish thought, as banging noises ricocheted from the boot. He needed to dump the body then drive as fast and as far away as he could.

He left the car in a lane that was dark and private, and found a window to break into. He jumped down into the concrete room and listened for her. He followed the creaking noise and when it suddenly stopped, she appeared before him, scaring the shit out of him with her screams.

The emotional outburst afterwards was unexpected, but he liked his girlfriends to have spirit, and she certainly had that now.

Why not? he thought to himself, as he jumped back out the window to empty the car. May as well have a bit of fun before heading off. After all, it's the middle of the night, the place will be deserted for hours. Plus, she's asking for it with that netball skirt. Every time she leans over you can make out her cunt.

43

It had taken Pete a while to convince the police that his anti-establishment, joyriding background did not automatically make him a serial killer. In fact, this argument didn't help at all, really, and if it hadn't been for his other arguments, he may never have been released.

The first argument concerned something Francesco had told him one night in the squat. Everyone was either watching hangover TV, or off sightseeing. Bronny and Hamish were 'doing London' which, he reflected, had taken them all of three hours.

'I just needed to check our availablity,' Francesco had told Pete in the kitchen. 'So I used my key to unlock the door to the Internet café and went in to use one of the computers. Hamish had left his terminal on. He wouldn't have expected anyone to go in, and I'm the only other person who has a key . . . Anyway, I changed the rates and then did what any normal person does, I had a sticky beak. Nothing unusual, I suppose, to have only visited porn sites in the last few days, but when I clicked on the images he'd saved, I realised this wasn't everyday stuff. Violent, quite specific. Would've taken him a while to collect.'

Francesco had apparently clicked on some of the images in his file: 'A runner who looked like she was being raped on an athletics track, an unhappy swimmer with goggles on her eyes and two penises in her mouth . . .'

Francesco and Pete had agreed that there was something very creepy about Hamish. Something intangible. He was slippery, and just as they were conferring, Hamish had slipped into the kitchen with Bronny, then slipped out again to watch TV.

But even though Francesco had confirmed this, it wasn't anything incriminating, not enough to convince the police of Pete's innocence. So Pete, tired and angry at having a leather gimp mask thrust in his face as some kind of confession aphrodisiac, asked if his DNA had been tested against samples from the leather gimp mask yet. They were working on it, and on DNA from the inside of his mouth, which would be tested against swabs taken from all over the scene, but it would take a while for the results. In the meantime, they agreed, that yes, if Pete donned gloves and a makeshift plastic head cover, he could try on the bloody leather gimp mask.

'If the glove don't fit, you have to acquit,' Pete said.

'Course it didn't fit. Pete had a large head. His mother had reminded him of this often, usually after her second glass.

Okay, so maybe he hadn't worn the mask, but maybe no one had – after all, the prints, blood and excrement on it had not been identified as yet. What else could they get on him? Time was running out. They had to find something.

And they did. In the afternoon, an officer went to his place of work and discovered a stolen purse in his locker.

'Some cleaners had it in for Bronwyn. They'd set her up,' Pete argued. 'I was just trying to help her. I snuck in, took it out of her locker and hid it. I was going to return it to the owner secretly, but she hadn't come back to the gym or steam rooms yet.'

'Why didn't you take it to the police?'

'I'm allergic.'

The officers then discovered why Pete was allergic to law enforcement. Since being deported from Australia six months earlier, he'd spent most of his time associating with shady types who might help him get home again.

'Why did you buy the fake passport?' Vera Oh asked.

'Because I wanted to go home,' Pete said, checking over his shoulder to see what she was looking at.

'Why did you jump the cruise ship in Morocco?'

'Because I wanted to get back to Australia.'

'Why did you fail to meet with your probation officer?'

'Because I had a meeting with someone who said he could help me get back to Australia.'

Day and night he'd been trying. He'd met more dodgy people-smugglers and identity salesmen than most criminals, and had spent all the money he'd earned on various attempts, none of which had worked. In fact, his ideas had all dried up and he was starting to think there was no way of getting home again.

But then he'd met Bronny and there was something about her, something that seemed as lost as he was. He loved the way she cared about plants and ate with gusto and how she said *okey-dokey* when she was nervous. He started to forget about the smell of the trees and the horizon that went everywhere and nowhere at the same time. She was very beautiful and she had no idea. Natural, like the country he loved, which wasn't over-groomed like the hedges and neat green fields of England. Unkempt almost. Dangerous almost. Raw, inhospitable, intangible and addictive.

Pete had never fallen in love before. He'd been too busy being angry – at his mother for being a drunk, at his father for being 12,000 miles away, at the world for thinking he was scum. He had no time for anything but anger and a drive in the dust under a huge open sky on a straight, flat road.

✧

The officers were starting to warm to him, he could tell, and when the other girl in the basement was identified as Leanne Donohue from Ballarat, they just about decided to let him go. Leanne Donohue had apparently fallen off a boat in Devon five months ago. She'd been with Hamish at the time – they'd done Europe together and were apparently great mates. Hamish had helped with the search, comforted the family. He'd even gone to Australia to attend her long awaited body-less memorial service. This trip had originally been Hamish's main alibi, but police soon discovered that he'd only been away for four days in total, and by the looks of Celia she'd been left alone for significant periods of time, so his holiday to Australia was no longer a viable defence.

Then there was the background report faxed in from Canada, completed after Hamish had been found guilty of a sexual assault charge during third year Computer Science at the University of Toronto . . .

Mr Watson has never had an intimate relationship with a woman. He admits to feelings of sexual inadequacy, saying he worries that he 'wouldn't function properly in that kind of situation'. He also displays callous sexual attitudes specifically targeted against women in their twenties and thirties. This callousness is evidenced in his description of the victim as 'a fit cunt'; as well as in his description of his mother when she was younger as 'the town whore'.

Mr Watson's mother, a drug user and single mother, abandoned her son while he was suffering from measles at the age of twelve. He was taken into care shortly after and has had no contact with his mother since.

Mr Watson also appears to view sex as an entitlement: 'She was wearing a tennis skirt two sizes too small!' He does not take responsibility for the offence, denying following the victim on several occasions before chasing her in the street and assaulting her.

In the writer's opinion, Mr Watson has no victim empathy, arguing 'she seemed to like it', and indeed feels he has been victimised himself – 'My life has been ruined by that slag . . .'

Just as Pete was about to be released, the hospital rang. 'She's awake!' the nurse said. 'The doctor's coming to check her and I've phoned Greg – he's on his way.'

Vera Oh bundled Pete into a police car and sped towards the hospital, rushing along corridors and up the stairs to the second floor. But they didn't find what they'd hoped to find – Celia awake and ready to identify her torturer. Instead they found Greg and his family wailing with grief in the waiting room.

44

Staring at the big eyes in the mirror, I realised that death had followed me. He had been with me on the plane, in transit, in the hostel, then under my bedroom. And he was here now, a guy with John Lennon glasses and a cute smile.

I tiptoed upstairs, checking to see if he was there. It was dark, so I couldn't tell if anyone was in the relaxation area, but it was quiet, so I kept walking as softly as I could past the loungers, through the double doors, past the kitchen, and into the reception booth. Assuming the emergency number was the same as at home, I dialled 000 – which didn't work. I tried it again, then again.

I heard a noise and hung up. Crawling out of the reception booth I found the front door and felt the lock, where I had left the key after arriving. It wasn't there.

I could hear the shower boiler creaking. There were other noises coming from downstairs. He must be down there again, I thought. I raced into the kitchen and grabbed the large knife I'd once used to chop toasted cheese sandwiches in half. I opened the double doors and entered the dark relaxation area. I crept across the marble tiles towards the internal door leading to the pool. The commotion downstairs was getting louder – a thud, another, another, banging, something being dragged along the floor, doors opening and closing. I hated to think what he might be doing down there. The internal door would not budge, and I remembered that it had been boarded and painted on the other side. I looked around the huge room. There were no windows, no escape routes. The only way, I realised, was through the window in the body-scrub room.

I moved towards the stairs, using the huge knife as my guide stick. I tiptoed past the tear-shaped plunge pool. Specks of light danced on the water. One by one I descended the stairs towards the shower area and body-scrub room.

The noises stopped before I had reached the bottom of the stairs. I stood still and listened. Was he coming? What could I do? I looked around for somewhere to hide, but there was nowhere to go and my reflection was bouncing from every mirror surrounding the pool. As I listened to his footsteps approaching, getting closer, I noticed the dark, quiet water of the plunge pool. I stepped into the freezing blackness, and slowly ducked my body and head under the water, trying not to make a splash or ripple. I held my breath with my eyes open. I could see he was walking right past me, up towards the relaxation area. I think I was crying underwater, my tears merging with it, my throat making a whale noise, a wet yell . . . and bubbles . . . shit, I was making bubbles, and I was running out of breath. I was going to get caught. He would drag me from the pool, get hold of my knife, and kill me.

Just in time, he disappeared from view.

Unable to hold my breath any longer, I came out of the water, took a huge breath, and raced from the pool, down the stairs, and into the body-scrub room. I ran over to the window, which had been open the last time I looked, but it was now nailed shut and there was no way of budging it.

I could hear him coming back down the stairs. I ran out into the shower area, turned towards the steam rooms and saunas, opened the door to the cleaning cupboard, shut it behind me, and tried to hide behind the broom-like *schmeissing* sticks in the corner.

He seemed to be checking the body-scrub room, checking the shower cubicles, one by one, checking the sauna that I'd unlocked earlier, and then walking towards the cupboard. He was opening the small metal door with the controls and keys in it, switching on all the switches, using the keys to unlock the other rooms. I could hear the mechanisms of the steam rooms bursting into action. I could see steam filtering in through the crack in the cupboard door. I held my hand over my mouth to stop any noise coming out, tears falling down my cheeks. Staying completely still, I watched as Hamish and a waft of steam entered the cupboard. I turned my head to the side as if this would help me be invisible.

The light in the cupboard came on.

'Hey you,' Hamish said, before picking up a tin and smashing it down on my head.

45

At the hospital, several different groups of people grappled with the change of circumstances. A nurse had been assaulted. Celia had been taken. Hamish Watson was a killer.

Vera Oh rang headquarters immediately, dispatching officers to the Royal, offering a description of the suspect, and ordering a nationwide alert.

No one in Celia's family could have imagined feeling worse than they had since their beloved had been taken. But they did feel worse. Their helpless grief was now topped with torture and madness. Greg prised himself away from his children. He asked his parents to take the crying boys home, and insisted on staying behind to help the police find his wife.

And Pete, free at last, grabbed the phone at the nurse's station to set about finding Bronny.

Phone call 1:

Pete: Francesco, pick up. Francesco.

Phone call 2:

Pete: Where are you?

Zach: In bed.

Pete: Have you seen Bronny?

Zach: Not since around nine. Far as I know, the girls all wanted to find somewhere else to stay.

Pete: Do you know where Francesco is?

Zach: No idea, mate.

Phone call 3:

Pete: Francesco, where the fuck are you?

Francesco: On the roof. The boss has given me some time off.

Pete: What's that grunting noise?

Francesco: Um, it's Melissa Jeffreys from Point Lons . . .Wo! .
. . dale.

Phone call 4:

Pete: Is Bronwyn Kelly there?

Mr Rutkowksi: Who?

Pete: Is Fliss there?

Mr Rutkowski: Fliss who?

Pete: Cheryl-Anne?

Mr Rutkowski: I don't know these people.

Phone call 5:

Pete: My name's Peter McGuire. I'm a friend of Bronwyn's.
I'm just wondering if you've heard from her?

Ursula: Yes, she rang. I've been waiting for her to call back.
Is she okay? We're worried about her.

Pete: Do you know where she was ringing from?

Urusla: No idea. I've been trying to find out. All I've got is a
fax and I can't trace it from here. She was just about to ring
the hospital.

Phone call 6:

Pete: . . . Do you know where she was ringing from?

Dr Gibbons: Actually I do. I called her back on . . . 020
75559083.

Pete: The Porchester . . .

Dr Gibbons: Sorry?

Pete: Nothing . . .

(A long beat).

Dr Gibbons: What?

Pete: . . . Was it yes or no?

✧

On Hamish's computer, the police found three sites he'd just visited – a 24-hour car-hire place, a booking site for P&O Ferries and an AA route planner from London to Dover.

In Hamish's bedroom they found the keys to the squat that Bronwyn had lost on the night of the squat-warming party, and a black bin bag of shitty clothes locked in a suitcase under the bed.

Vera Oh felt like shit. She'd never removed Greg from her suspect list, always thought it might be the bastard husband because she had a thing about bastard husbands. Even as she interrogated Peter McGuire, she continued to think Greg might have killed his wife. After all, she was experienced enough to recognise that Pete might just be a young rogue who was teetering on the edge of growing up.

But she didn't have time to dwell on her feelings of guilt because she knew who the killer was now, and it seemed clear that at some time after 9 p.m. he had headed to Dover in a red Fiat.

46

When I woke up I was lying on the floor of the cupboard. Hamish had taken his drenched T-shirt off me – it was on the floor beside me – and had changed me into my underwear, netball skirt and polo shirt.

Earlier, when I'd looked in the mirror and seen the big eyes on the T-shirt, I'd reverted to my former terrified self. I'd run away, hid. But when I woke up in the cupboard and thought about him touching me, dressing me; when I thought about how he'd been my best friend, how he'd given me money and peanut butter, gone to London Bridge with me and Oxford; when I thought about how his pointy little face had irked me on the plane when he'd spoken those very first words: 'You should never tell a man you've had too much to drink,' I realised that I did not want to hide or run away. I wanted to kill him.

I could hear him making more commotion – what the fuck was he doing? I crept out of the cupboard and headed towards the noise, which was coming from one of the saunas. The doors to the steam rooms were open and the entire floor was now filled with hot steam. I could hardly see a thing. I walked determinedly towards the room he was in and shut the door of the sauna behind me.

He still hadn't heard me. I moved within inches of his back and saw that he was putting gloves on. He turned. We looked at each other.

I don't know what I thought I was going to do, exactly, but I thought my bare hands would suffice, and I didn't expect him to be stronger than me. When I lunged at him, he pushed me to the ground and sat on my stomach, his legs pinning down my arms. I kicked my knees into his back, again and again, and his legs jolted so that my arms became free. I grabbed his face and head, using my unfiled nails to tear at his cheeks and eyes. I pulled hard at his bottom lip, trying to rip it right off his face. I punched his glasses so that they smashed and fell to the floor.

He managed to stand, and began kicking me in the side.

'This isn't you, Hamish,' I said between groans. 'Hamish? Let me go, and I won't tell anyone. I won't tell the police.'

I was lying, of course. I was still determined to kill him.

'Really?' he asked.

'I promise.'

Then he kicked me for so long that I thought I would die.

✧

Coming to, I realised I was slumped on the lower wooden bench of the sauna, right beside the hot coals. Hamish was yanking my hair so hard with his left hand that I felt he might rip my head off. He was standing over me with his trousers around his knees. He'd locked the door, leaving the key in the lock. The coals were burning hot beside my right foot. The tin Hamish had hit me with was next to the coals. Hamish held his flaccid penis in his other hand.

'The police will be looking for you,' I said.

'Maybe, but no one will come near here till morning so I'm having what you might call a leaving party.'

Hamish was hard now. I shut my eyes and prayed for him to disappear, but when I opened my eyes, he was still there, still pulling himself, still pulling the hair from my head.

'Please, stop!' I begged, to which he moved his pathetic little pelvis back and forward mid-air. I twisted, kicked and punched as much as I could. I wanted to vomit. I wanted to cry. I *was* crying. He was licking my forehead now. My eyes were scrunched closed and tears were flowing down my face.

I turned my face to the side, looked out towards the thick steam, opened my eyes, and saw a ghost. Dressed in white. Pressing its face against the glass. I stared at it silently, wondering if maybe I'd died already. If I had, I hadn't gone to heaven.

47

Celia had thought — as he wheeled her at scalpel-point to the car — this could not be happening. She'd been saved, hadn't she? Hadn't she been spared? Wasn't she on the brink of getting her life back?

She decided to play dead. It wasn't so hard, seeing as most of her face was covered with bandages. All she had to do was hold her breath in his presence. So that's what she did. When he pulled the handle to the boot, she held her breath and kept her eyes wide open. She tried not to show emotion or movement in her eyes as she saw his face for the first time. Just a pointy nerd with no chin. An insignificant squiggle of a man. He looked flustered, had a lot on his plate, and so he didn't check her very carefully, just picked her tiny frame up, tossed her through a high, open window, and left her where she landed, on the floor of a concrete room. She tried to remain calm as he came in through the window after her, and then nailed the window shut.

A noise upstairs made him stop, listen, and then leave. After he disappeared out the door, Celia thought hard. She didn't have the energy to walk. She knew she wouldn't get far. She would have to hide. She crawled over to the concrete slab, which was held up by two large boards, and slid in between them. Celia ripped the surgical tape from her mouth and thought hard about her next move.

A girl ran in and then out. Celia crawled from underneath the concrete slab towards the steamy doorway. She wondered which way would save her, and turned left. She was crawling at a snail's pace, hoping there would be a door or a window or a telephone nearby, when a gust of air cleared the steam for a moment and a closed glass room came into view.

The girl was in there. She recognised her now. It was the girl who'd found her in the basement. The girl who she'd tried to contact for days on end, who had talked in her sleep and played the Beatles. It was the girl who'd come to save her, who'd held her and cried, who'd reminded her of the boys and begged her to live.

The girl was cowering as the man held her hair and rubbed himself in front of her face. Celia looked ahead of her – she should crawl away. She should hide again.

She couldn't. On all fours, she moved towards the sauna an inch at a time, her breathing laboured, and when she finally reached it, she banged on the glass with her good hand. She tried to yell and eventually managed a tiny mouse-squeak that no one would ever hear.

'Leave her alone! Bastard! Leave her alone!'

48

Bronny could make out Celia's beautiful crying eyes. She was banging on the glass but not making any sound. Hamish hadn't noticed. He was too busy yanking at himself.

'Shhh!' she gestured to Celia with her mouth and eyes, and Celia stopped banging for a second.

Hamish was nearly there, so he kept saying, nearly there.

Bronny mouthed 'Police' to Celia, but soon realised she couldn't ring the police. The phone was miles away, upstairs. She didn't know where, and she couldn't even stand up.

Nearly there, nearly there.

There were only two possible outcomes, Bronny realised. Hamish would either kill her, or kill her *and* Celia.

She used all her strength to free herself from Hamish's grasp, race to the door, grab the key, and push it under the glass. She and Hamish were locked inside.

Celia was safe now.

'Jesus Christ!' Hamish yelled. 'What the fuck!'

Hamish tried to open the door, but couldn't. He beat at the glass with his fists. It shook, as if it might shatter at any moment.

Bronny grabbed him to stop him from smashing the glass. He turned, pushed her down onto the bench and began to squeeze the air from her throat with both hands.

Gasping for breath while looking directly at him, Bronny took her right hand, reached down, and took hold of a burning coal. It sizzled into her palm and though a wave of agony juddered through her, her hatred was more powerful than the pain. She pushed the contents of her smouldering palm against Hamish's bare groin. The coal hisssed as it stuck to the skin of his penis.

He let go of her throat, screamed, immobilised: a possum electrocuted on a power-line.

'Hang on,' Bronny rasped, 'I'm nearly there. Nearly there.'

As she pressed harder, his penis fused with his testicles, the smell of burning flesh rising with his screams.

His dick flattened to overdone.

'NOOOO!' he screamed.

'Yes,' she said. 'Yes, yes.'

Prising her melted skin from his, Bronny flicked the coal away and put her hand in the bucket of water.

Hamish fell and rolled around on the floor, yelling. After a moment, he began edging his way towards the glass again, screaming, smashing at it with his hands and legs. Bronwyn no longer had the strength to stop him.

The glass cracked.

Bronny realised she could not overwhelm him. She noticed the tin Hamish had hit her with next to her right foot. She looked at it properly for the first time – it was rat poison.

Another fracture appeared in the glass wall. One more thump and he would be able to kill Celia and her.

Taking off the lid, Bronny tilted the open tin of liquid poison over the coals and roared: 'Move and I'll let it go!'

Hamish turned and looked. It took him a moment, and then his eyes registered.

'You wouldn't,' he said.

She could see Celia on the floor outside, lying down, eyes barely open. She could see Hamish daring her, not believing her.

'You're too afraid.'

Bronny tilted the poison. A drip landed beside the coals.

She smiled, because an hour ago, Hamish would have been right. She would have been scared – of test results, of ordering drinks on planes, of roller-coasters and heights and . . .

She smiled, because that was an hour ago.

Hamish smashed the glass, harder this time, and the fractures expanded.

Bronny tilted the tin. The liquid oozed onto the coals, spitting and spluttering a dirty yellow steam which rose up to enter their throats like cut glass.

Hamish and Bronny fell to the floor.

⚬

She'd thought a lot about the actual moment.

She'd imagined yelling in anger to stop the pain, screaming 'No!' or 'More morphine!' or 'Help me, help me! Please, please, for God's sake, help me!'

She'd imagined seeing a light and reaching out her hand with a weirdly contented expression on her face.

She'd imagined embarrassing herself with a grey unflattering bra and shitty underpants that did not match.

She'd imagined embracing Catholicism at the last moment, just in case.

She'd imagined flashes of her life zooming past like trucks overtaking her car window on the freeway.

She'd imagined floating above herself and looking down to a bed surrounded by doctors and nurses and crying people.

She'd imagined calling the last of a long line of people into the room and telling them it's okay and that she'd always be with them, in a way.

She'd imagined calling the first of only a short line of people into the room but being told by a scary nurse that the person had nipped out to the milk bar to get eggs.

She'd imagined being overcome with tremors of terror that this was it, this was death, it was coming, and nothing she could do would stop it.

The moment had come and she didn't want to grab or yell or scream or hold her hand to the light and she didn't feel terrified or think about final speeches. She was too busy coughing, and if she hadn't been too busy coughing, the only thing she'd have wanted to do was cry.

Gathering her upper half into a foetal position and drawing her wide-open knees as close to her chest as possible, Bronny saw a tiny scar on her left knee. She'd never noticed it before – must've been from that trike accident when she was three.

49

Vera Oh dropped Pete at the front entrance to the Porchester. It looked like the bastard was heading for France.

'Don't worry, we'll get him,' she said, feeling confident that they had their man, that they would find him, save Celia, and that no one else would get hurt.

Pete leapt out of the police car and ran towards the door to the Porchester. The doctor hadn't told him, but he could tell from his voice that it was yes. The poor girl, she had it. Pete was glad, at least, that she had found somewhere safe to hide, and prayed as he ran that she would still be there so he could hold her, hug her, tell her it would be okay. Not only would they find a way to deal with it together, but they would have at least twenty years of love and happiness, more than most people get in a lifetime.

Pete picked the lock and went inside. It was dark, and he couldn't hear anything.

'Bronny?' he yelled.

Pete felt the soil of the bamboo palm. It was wet. She was here.

'Bron, I know you've spoken to the doctor. Where are you?'

He looked in the kitchen – no one was there. He walked through the double doors, down past the plunge pool, down the stairs. The place was filled with steam.

'Bronny! Where are you?'

He walked towards the steam rooms and tripped over. When he stood up, he realised he'd fallen over a woman.

He knelt down and rolled her onto her back, recognising immediately that it was Celia. He gasped, knowing this meant Hamish was here, that Bronny was in danger. Checking her pulse, Pete carried Celia upstairs as quietly as possible. He put her in the reception booth in the recovery position, satisfied that she was breathing, and rang the police.

Pete ran into the relaxation area, then downstairs through the mist and looked into steam room 1, steam room 2, sauna 1 . . . then sauna 2. The door was closed, and Bronwyn and Hamish were in spasms on the floor.

50

The Sick Man felt very sick. He thought back to when he'd been ill as a boy, and his mother had trickled water from a flannel onto his forehead. It had felt good. The sound was soothing. She might have smiled at him. He couldn't remember, but he liked to think she had.

A trickle of water was what he needed, just as he had after days of crippling agony, of listening to every noise at the door, of watching outside to see if she was coming home. Was that her? Coming home? No, it wasn't. It was a postman, a girl jogging – an okay feeling for a moment – another postman, and another, social services, not a trickle.

He'd felt sick ever since, except for the occasional moment, but never as sick as he'd felt in his twelve-year-old self's bedroom, not even now. Not even now, lying on the floor of a sauna that had steam made of razor blades slashing your bleeding innards.

Could he please hear it now? Not the coughing and the banging and the yelling. Not the shattering of glass and the scream, but the trickling of water from a flannel to a forehead?

Could he?

Please?

51

Pete had lost everything. At birth, his mother, to drink. At five, his father, to England. At twenty-four his country, to cars. And now . . .

Like all those other times, he knew he was powerless to stop it. Like when the yelling got so bad his Dad called a taxi, hugged him at the door, cried, and said: 'There's nothing else I can do, son. I'll visit.'

Like when his Mum had peed herself while he microwaved two packets of real beef lasagne.

Like when the need to say *fuck you* had gotten so desperate that he'd smashed a window with his bare fist and punched an officer with the same hand.

So he was used to losing things. But as he washed water over Bronwyn, hoping the toxins would leave her body, he prayed for the ambulance to be fast, please God, because he didn't want to have to *lose* again, didn't want to have to recover, get tougher, again.

○

Vera Oh had been heading south at high speed when the call came in. She said fuck, then shit, then swerved full pelt across the motorway.

'Fuck, shit and fuck,' she said, taking out an emergency cigarette from her glove compartment, lighting it, and sucking the guilt into her lungs. It was her fault, wasn't it? She'd had him in the cell, the weed. Had questioned him at length, and ignored a gut feeling that it might be him – something about the way he had all the right answers ready.

'It's just a feeling,' she'd admitted to her fellow interrogator. 'Nothing concrete.' And with continuing suspicions about the husband, and with Peter McGuire and his leather gimp mask *in situ*, she'd let him go.

'Shit, fuck, shit, fuck, shit, fuck, shit,' she continued, lighting the second emergency cigarette.

'You're only supposed to have one,' her police passenger remarked, returning the Silk Cuts to the glove compartment.

'Fuck, fuck, fuck,' was her answer.

When Vera finally arrived at the entrance to the baths, five other police vehicles were already there, along with two ambulances.

'Inside,' someone yelled.

Vera ran towards the corner door.

52

The last few weeks don't flash before me, they amble. I'm touching the rough face of a beautiful man. I'm losing my shoe on a London roof. I'm being carried on a Singapore conveyor belt. I'm sitting on top of the world watching Australia go on and on beneath me. I'm running away from the hospital.

And now I'm running towards my home. Mr Todd, caked in cracked dirt, is riding one of his horses out of the old railway, smiling. The pigs are scampering onto the street from the bacon factory, wriggling their ears. Ursula and Dad are on the veranda, waving at me as I run towards them. My steps are getting bigger. They're huge and fast and high, so high that, just when I think I'm going to land on the veranda, I fly right past and land several feet on the other side. I turn and jump back towards Dad and Ursula again, but it's like I'm slowly crawling up the hill of the Scenic Railway and when I hurtle back down, I land even further on the other side. They're looking up at me now. I must be thirty feet up in the air, yelling at them as I come down to land at least sixty feet away from them this time.

I breathe. I've been dunked in the freezing plunge pool and Pete's embracing me, crying, and saying, look at me, hold on, hold on. I can see Vera Oh. I can see Greg smiling down at me: 'Thank you, Celia's alive, she's okay, thank you, thank you,' he says.

'I love you,' Pete whispers.

I know exactly how to respond . . .

'I want you to come home with me. Do you understand?'

He nods, and locks his fingers with mine. A man who loves me is holding my hand as I die.

Greg disappears to go to Celia.

I close my eyes. Pete has joined Ursula and Dad on the veranda. They're getting smaller and smaller, so teensy as I leap back and forth.

I can't see them at all now.

Is that a trike?

The bounding is starting to feel exhilarating.

I find myself yelling: '*Wheeeee!*

Thanks to my editor, Alison Rae at Polygon, and to my early twenties, which I somehow survived.

H.F.